Smith's MONTHLY

Every Month Original Novels, Stories, and Articles

USA Today Bestselling Writer **Dean Wesley Smith**

TABLE OF CONTENTS

SMITH'S MONTHLY ISSUE #25

All Contents copyright © 2015 Dean Wesley Smith
Published by WMG Publishing
Cover and interior design copyright © 2015 WMG Publishing

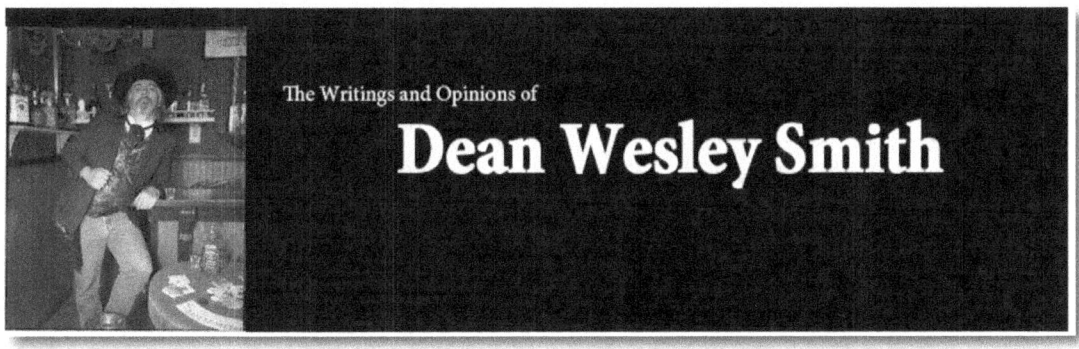

The Writings and Opinions of
Dean Wesley Smith

Introduction
THE TALE OF THREE BOOKS

In this first issue of the third year of *Smith's Monthly*, two events are happening at the same time.

The first event is that the eighth and last installment of the novel *An Easy Shot* is in this issue.

An Easy Shot has a back story. It was first published in a very different form under another name and under one of my pen names.

When the publisher decided to shut down, they did the very honorable thing and reverted all rights to the authors of all the books they had published, or had under contract.

In this modern world, that is almost unheard of.

I had no plan of ever bringing this novel back into print. I had written it specifically for that publisher and they had treated it very well. In fact, as with most of my novels from those years, I had just

forgotten it. Then a friend told me about how she had indie published her novel from that same publisher and her readers seemed to be enjoying it.

So since that press had a very clear slant that I wrote the novel to fill, I started back through the novel, bringing it up to speed, writing a bunch new every month, changing the slant, and finally giving this novel a new life, one month at a time over the last eight months.

So two things allowed this to happen.

First, a very generous original publisher who reverted the rights when I requested them. And secondly, this new publishing world that allows me to do this magazine every month now for twenty-five months.

At some point down the road, I will put the entire novel together in one issue, but for the moment, the thriller is finally done after eight months.

Second event in this issue is the publication of the novel *Star Mist: A Seeders Universe Novel*. *Star Mist* stands alone

---

Thanks for the Support

Dean Wesley Smith

just fine as a novel, but it is also clear that the problem the characters in the novel are facing continues far beyond the last page.

The problem actually will continue for a second novel, *Star Rain* in the next issue. Just as the Seeders universe is huge, this two-book series covers a massive event in an already massive universe.

So as one serial ends, two novels start that can be looked at as one big story as well.

I sure hope you enjoy the novels as much as I enjoyed writing them.

And I hoped you enjoyed *An Easy Shot*.

Next month, I will be starting a brand new serial novel, plus a writing series.

Of course, every issue will have all the short fiction as well.

Thanks for the support of this wild and crazy project. I'm sure having fun and I hope, as this magazine heads into its third year, you will stick with me. The ride has just begun.

—Dean Wesley Smith
October 3, 2015
Lincoln City, Oregon

#22...July 2015

#23...August 2015

#24...September 2015

#25...October 2015

Coming Next Issue in Smith's Monthly
STAR RAIN
A Seeders Universe Novel

Smith's MONTHLY

NUMBER TWENTY-SIX
NOVEMBER, 2015

*Original Stories,
Novels, and Articles*

DEAN WESLEY SMITH
STAR RAIN
A Seeders Universe Novel

Missing! Laverne, Lady Luck herself.

Poker Boy, Front Desk Girl, and Screamer chase after every lead, as well as every other Gambling God and hero in the gambling universe. The three of them get to the truth of what happened to Laverne.

But saving the world from unraveling? Without luck, they may not have the time.

LUCK BE A LADY
A Poker Boy Story

ONE

ONE NIGHT, while playing in a great, no-limit game, I was asked if I believed in luck. I said, "Sure, I've met her." That got a laugh and the subject changed.

Now understand that professional poker players like me tend to really downplay the factor of luck in our sport, using the great old saying, "It will all even out."

I have to admit that I agree with that, even though I sometimes wonder why luck exists at all when a bad player hits a two-outer to beat me out of a few hundred bucks. Particularly when I know I had the best hand going to the last card, and ninety-four-point-four percent of the time I will win that same hand. Correct as far as the math goes, but not very comforting as I watch the idiot player pull my money toward him.

Most people would say in those circumstances that I was unlucky and the idiot was lucky. I never looked at it that way. I just repeated, "It will all even out," as if I didn't really believe in luck.

I have to admit, I've hit my share of two-outers over the years against other players. But as Poker Boy, one of the only superheroes in the Poker World, I try not to get into hands where the only way I can win is hit one of two cards left in the deck that could win the hand for me. It is just too embarrassing.

So, do I actually believe in luck? Like I said, sure. I've met her. And I'm not kidding. And she scared hell out of me.

Her name is Laverne, and she runs everything. She's the top Gambling God, the CEO of all gambling of all types, including risks in business, health, sports, and life in general. She's the one woman in the world you would not want mad at you.

I met her right after the big problems with the Ghost Slot machines. She is what you would imagine Lady Luck to be: short, but powerful, brown hair pulled back, with brown eyes that see through everything. She is completely in control of all the Gods of Gambling. She flat scared me speechless when she thanked Front Desk Girl, my sidekick, and me. She said we did a "damn fine" job in rescuing the gambling industry. Then she smiled.

Those who wish "Lady Luck to smile on them" have never actually had it happen. I was trembling so hard that all I could do was nod and just try to stammer out a "Thanks."

Stan, the God of Poker and my boss, later told me I did just fine. He told me he gets scared every time he has to meet Laverne as well. Usually he just reports to Burt, the God of Casino Operations, who is his boss and second in command of all Gambling Gods under Laverne.

I had hoped to never have a reason to meet Laverne again. I had no idea how long superheroes in the gambling industry lived, but no matter how long it was going to be for me, I did not want to end up in that office of hers again. However,

like any poker player, I kept hoping she would "smile" on me every so often from a distance, especially when I stumbled into one of those two-outer situations on the wrong side.

But distance from Lady Luck wasn't to be an option for me.

It was a calm Christmas Eve.

Christmas Eve always tends to bring me strange problems to solve, weird people to rescue, and once even an old girlfriend with new boobs that she thought aliens wanted. So, wouldn't you just know that it would be on Christmas Eve that the biggest problem of my short 42 years would come calling.

It was around six-thirty, and I had just finished some darned fine turkey with dressing and gravy in the casino buffet, after which I sat down in a really nice three/five no limit cash game. I lived in a manufactured home about a half-mile from the Native American casino I liked to call my "home casino." and when home I always ate at the casino, usually in the buffet. For some reason, the cooks there were just better than even my ability to microwave a Hungry Man dinner.

On Christmas Eve in a casino, it is usually only the hardcore players, and this Christmas was no exception. About fourteen guys and two women crowded around two of the eleven poker tables. I would have bet that not a one of us had much family, and clearly none of us had anything better to do on a very cold and damp Tuesday night in December in Oregon.

I had just picked up a pair of nines in late position behind three players who had already limped in. There was just not much for me to do with those cards in that position except call and hope to hit a set. If I tried raising with the nines, anyone who would call me would surely have me beat. But if I got in cheap and hit a third nine on the flop, I could make a bunch of money. So, as I tossed a five dollar chip out in front of me, I felt a hand on my shoulder and glanced up.

It was Stan, the God of Poker.

Now, the last thing you need on a calm Christmas Eve after a good turkey dinner is the God of Poker standing behind you not looking happy. All I could think about was that I had somehow screwed up rescuing that woman with big hair and an even bigger dog a few days before. I had managed to get her professional help right before she started stealing funds from the school where she was the book-keeper to pay for her poker debt. She was, without a doubt, the worst poker player I had ever met. Everything she knew about the game she had learned by watching late night poker on television. To her, a seven-deuce off-suit was as powerful as a pair of kings, and she always got angry when she lost with that combination, which was most every time she played.

I just hoped she wasn't back in a poker room again.

"After the hand," Stan said, "a word."

Everyone at the table glanced up at Stan, then just looked away. They had no idea who they were looking at, and that he was the guy they were always asking for help or being angry at. More than likely Stan had some sort of "don't pay attention to me" shield up.

I nodded, glanced back at the flop to see that no nine had hit the table, then stood, leaving my cards face down in front of my spot with a nod at the dealer to fold them out when it came around to my turn. I quickly grabbed my chips and stuffed them in my pocket. If Stan had come to get me, chances are it was going

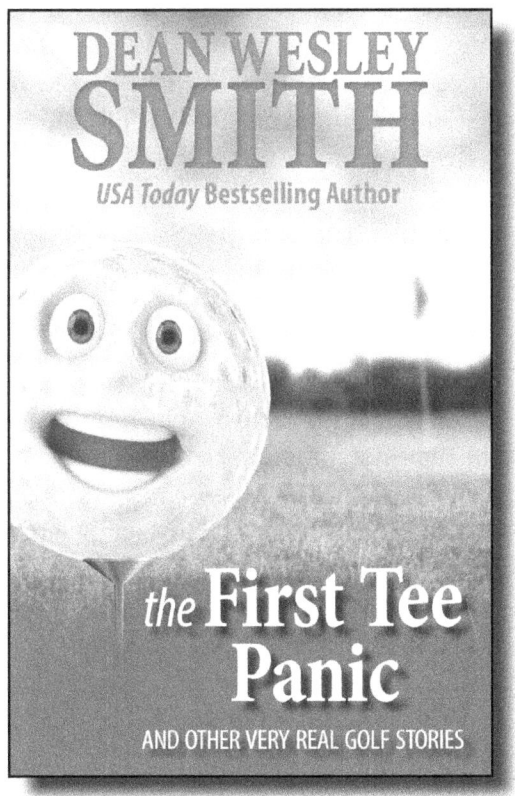

to be a little while before I returned to the game.

I zipped up my superhero uniform as I followed Stan toward the poker room front door. My uniform is a short, black leather jacket and a fedora-like golf hat. Both allow me to take my superhero energy from any casino I am in or near. I had a hunch that Stan coming to get me meant I was going to need just about all my powers. In all the years I had worked for him, he had never done this.

Ever.

Normally I just stumbled into the people who needed my help. And if I needed to talk to Stan, I went to find him.

Something was really wrong.

As we stepped out of the poker room and into the larger casino area, my hometown casino just faded away and I suddenly found myself in Stan's office. Out his big picture window, the lights of Vegas lit up the Christmas Eve sky. I loved Vegas. I just hadn't expected to be here at the moment.

And I didn't expect Patty Ledgerwood, a.k.a. Front Desk Girl, to stand and greet me as well. She looked like she had just come from a corporate business meeting, with a fashionable brown pantsuit over a white blouse. Simple pearls were all that she wore for jewelry, and she had her long brown hair down and combed perfectly. Stunning was the only way to describe her, and my breath just caught in my throat like I had caught a pair of aces playing head's up late in a tournament.

She gave me a huge and long hug, and I have to admit, I returned the hug, getting lost in her long brown hair and her wonderful smell of apricots. Since the big affair with the Ghost Slots, Patty and I had been an item, a couple, good friends, and great partners in a number of other adventures. Clearly Stan figured whatever was wrong was going to need us both again.

"Merry Christmas," she said, giving me that beaming smile that made my knees weak as she pushed me out to arm's length. For a moment I got lost in her big brown eyes, then she kissed me.

Right there in front of the God of Poker.

I didn't care. I kissed her back. Christmas Eve was looking up, that was for sure.

Suddenly I wished I hadn't zipped up my leather jacket. Warm wasn't half of what I was feeling right at that moment.

"Excuse me," Stan said, dropping into his chair with a look of amusement on his face as we pulled apart, "but we have a problem that could use you two."

He pointed to the chairs in front of his desk and we sat. But I didn't let go of her hand. Patty and I had a real connection, even so much that we could stop time around us, using parts of both of our powers to do it. Besides, I just liked the feel of her skin against mine and couldn't believe a woman as good looking as she was would even be interested in a poker player like me.

"Okay, right to the point," Stan said, suddenly very serious. "Laverne is missing."

That was such a stupid statement, I just snorted, not a very appealing sound, but one that suited such an absurd statement.

"Now, seriously," Patty said, letting go of my hand and leaning in toward Stan. "What exactly is going on?"

Stan didn't blink, and I couldn't get a read on him in any way. He was the God of Poker after all, and had the best poker face that ever existed.

"Not kidding, I'm afraid," he said. "Laverne has gone missing. As of two hours and six minutes ago real time, there has been no such thing as luck, either good or bad, in the world."

Patty opened her pretty mouth, then closed it without saying a word. I just sat back and stared at Stan. There was no reason at all he would play some sort of prank on us on Christmas Eve, let alone suggest such a thing as Lady Luck herself being missing. Such a thing could get even the God of Poker fired.

But to be honest, in my lowly position as a superhero in the gambling world, I had no idea who might be more powerful than Laverne. I had heard about Karen, Stew, and Mickey, the Gods of Death, Dying, and Spirits; but unless Laverne's time had come to leave this planet, I couldn't imagine those three being involved.

And way back in time there used to be a guy called Zeus who had other names down through time, but he was officially retired and out of the game.

Hell, Laverne had been around since the time of the Greeks and way before. Over the centuries she had taken over all of gambling. From what I had heard, she had gained power over the last few centuries until she was now one of the most powerful of them all. Even all the sports gods, financial gods, and health gods now reported to her.

About the only gods who outranked her now were The Powers That Be and the Fates. I had no doubt that someone far above me would be contacting them pretty soon, if this didn't get cleared up.

"Why do you say missing?" Patty asked. "Did she maybe just go on vacation?"

"My bosses are calling it a kidnapping," Stan said. "But I'm not so sure about that. She is missing and they are panicked, to be honest with you. Even the Fates are stumped. And since you two did such a good job on the Ghost Slot problem, Burt wants you both in on this as well, even though every god above you is also working on this."

"You don't expect much out of us, I hope," I said.

He shrugged but didn't disagree. Always better to keep a boss's expectations low; then when something works out, you look even better.

I wanted to ask him what he thought a couple of lowly superheroes could do to find Lady Luck herself. Stan knew the odds, and without luck playing a part in anything at the moment, it was only odds that ruled the world. Simple odds. And the odds in this case were not with Patty and me.

Suddenly it dawned on me what I had thought.

Odds.

I needed someone to compute straight computer odds on exactly where Laverne might be, and I knew exactly who could do it.

I sat back, thinking, as Patty asked Stan another question.

"What's going to happen to the world without luck?" Patty asked.

"No one really knows," Stan said. "It's been a part of human nature since the beginning of time."

"I'm betting it's going to get real boring," I said.

Patty and Stan both nodded to that.

TWO

ONE HOUR LATER, Patty and I sat in a small diner just down the street from Binion's Hotel and Casino in downtown Las Vegas. One street over, the light show along Freemont was going full force for those out on Christmas Eve, but inside the café it was just the two of us.

Our gum-popping waitress, Madge, had on her usual too-tight brown uniform with a stained apron over the front. On my first visit to this café, I had learned to never look at Madge as she walked away. Let's just say she wore underwear of the type that not even a skinny woman could be comfortable in. And Madge was far from thin, no matter how small a uniform she jammed herself into every day.

The Diner was one of those tossbacks to the 1950s and early 1960s, with phony decorations and everything in red and black checks, including the tile on the floor and the booths. It just glared pretend memories. I didn't need to pretend to have memories—I had enough real ones of my own.

The minute we had dropped into a booth, I had used Patty's cell phone to call the third member of our superhero trio. Screamer, a guy who could take the thoughts out of one person's mind and let another person see them. He also could roam around inside a person's head on touch, and make them see things they didn't want to see. He got his nickname from making a mass-murderer scream so loud that the murderer damaged his vocal cords and had to write down where he had buried ten different bodies. Screamer often worked with the Las Vegas police and casino owners.

I just had a gut feeling that we were going to need him.

When I had told Screamer that Patty and I had an important case, he had said. "At The Diner?"

"Yup," I had said.

"Be there in ten minutes." Not even one complaint about it being Christmas Eve.

For over five cases now, since the great Ghost Slots case, we had used The Diner as a meeting place. It was like a second home for all three of us in Vegas.

No one was on The Diner's five slots tonight, which for some reason made me feel a little better about humanity in general. Usually the elderly played those slots at all times of the day or night, pumping away their retirement savings simply because they had nothing better to do with their time. Hitting a small jackpot gave them a moment of excitement, a feeling of youth for a fleeting second before the bell stopped and the machine asked for another dollar.

At least tonight, on this one special night, they had something else to do for a few hours. Chances are some of them would be back tomorrow.

Patty and I decided to split a chocolate milkshake, since the milkshakes here were large enough to send a normal person into a diabetic coma. Patty had had dinner at the Mirage earlier with her father, and my wonderful turkey and gravy from the buffet was still keeping me satisfied. Madge had just brought the shake when Screamer came in and dropped into the booth beside Patty.

Screamer's real name was Toledo Moss, and he looked like any other tourist you would see walking the Strip, with his short cut brown hair, his dark glasses, his loud Hawaiian shirt, Bermuda shorts, and sandals.

Screamer had lived in Vegas his entire life and knew exactly how to blend in. No one looking at any of us sitting in that booth would think we were three superheroes, fighting to help the weak, and this time bring luck back to the planet.

"I'm hearing rumors that something big is going on," Screamer said turning back to face me after he asked Madge for his own chocolate shake.

"Laverne is missing," Patty said.

Screamer snorted, just as I had done, then laughed. I'm glad I wasn't the only one who snorted at the news.

"Stan told us a few minutes before I called you," I said. "She's been missing for two and a half hours now."

Screamer stared at me, then glanced at Patty to see her serious face before turning back to face me across the booth. "Is luck missing as well?"

I nodded. "Completely, from the entire world, from what Stan said."

Screamer opened his mouth, then closed it, clearly stunned.

We all sat there for a long minute, just thinking, until finally Screamer said, "I can't imagine the world without luck."

I shrugged. "Since I'm a poker player and don't believe in luck, I can imagine it just fine. Everything will just continue to happen as it statistically should."

Screamer again started to say something, then smiled and stared right at me. "Poker Boy, I can tell you have a plan."

"Read me like a book," I said, smiling back. "First off, we need to figure out who would get the most out of Lady Luck, and all luck for that matter, being gone. Who would have the power to trick or trap Laverne and hold her, and gain by doing so?"

"Not many, I would guess," Patty said.

"That's what we need to find out," I said.

Patty and Screamer both nodded so I went on. "Second, we need to find out statistically what the chances are for different causes of Laverne's vanishing. Since luck is no longer with us, only numbers will dictate what happened—or will happen—to her."

"And how are we going to do that?" Screamer asked.

"Oh, don't tell me," Patty said, staring at me, looking disgusted.

I didn't blame her. Just the idea had me feeling a little nauseous, but I could see no choice. "The Bookkeeper."

"Oh, no chance," Screamer said, shaking his head from side to side. "I'd rather crawl around in a mass murderer's head than go into that house again."

"I'll do it," I said, sounding a lot more sure of myself than I actually did. The Bookkeeper was the most brilliant statistician in history, and a superhero over in the mathematics world of gods. He had been around and working for the gods for centuries. However, he looked very much like a rat, and his house smelled so bad that last time I went in there I had to stand in a shower for an hour to even pretend to get the smell off of me.

"Good," Screamer said. "I'll start asking around about who had it out for Laverne, who was feuding with her, that sort of thing."

"I'll go with you," Patty said to me, "but I'm changing into old clothes first."

"Thanks," I said. "We're a long-shot on solving this."

"Not as long a shot as you might think," Screamer said. "The three of us are a pretty powerful team."

I could only nod at that, but I still didn't believe we had much of a chance. We were only lowly superheroes. Lady Luck was one of the top gods of all gods. And without luck, who knew what would happen.

Screamer stood and tossed a five on the table to pay for the milkshake Madge hadn't delivered yet. "I'll get going, see what I can dig up, meet you two back here? How long?"

"Three hours," I said. "We'll need time for showers."

"Good luck out there." He turned and headed for the door.

Patty and I sat, just enjoying each other's company as we finished our milkshake and part of Screamer's. Neither of us was in a real hurry to wade into that smell that filled The Bookkeeper's home.

THREE

PATTY CHANGED CLOTHES while I waited in the car outside of her condo, not really wanting to chance going upstairs and getting distracted. Twenty minutes later, we pulled up in front of the dark house belonging to The Bookkeeper.

It was a standard, suburban house in a pretty standard subdivision. Only unlike the others along the street, his house had no landscaping at all, just weeds and covered-over windows. The house had tall fences on both sides, built by the neighbors to shut off the look of the house from the rest of the homes along the silent street. Christmas decorations lit up most of the homes, looking odd in the desert climate. Only The Bookkeeper's house had no decorations, and clearly hadn't been painted in decades.

Now Available
from all your favorite booksellers in trade paper and electronic editions.

COLD CALL

A COLD POKER GANG MYSTERY

DEAN WESLEY SMITH

USA TODAY BESTSELLING AUTHOR

I left my hat and coat in the car, not wanting to get my superhero costume smelling so much I couldn't wear it again. I had other black coats and other hats that worked just as well as a superhero costume, but they were back in Oregon in my double-wide trailer near the casino. Luckily I had left a few changes of regular clothes, including another pair of shoes, in Patty's apartment a month or so back, so I could change everything but my coat and hat after we were finished here.

About halfway up the sidewalk on this warm Christmas Eve, the smell started to hit us, and by the time we were standing at the door, my eyes were watering.

Let me try to describe this smell. Imagine a full garbage can behind a fish restaurant sitting in the sun for a few days, then combine that with a dirty cat box that hadn't been changed for a month, and mix in a full latrine stench.

Yeah, bad didn't begin to describe it.

"You don't need to do this," I said to Patty, trying to cover my nose with my arm but failing miserably.

"I have a hunch this is going to need us both," Patty said, blinking hard and clearly trying to not choke.

I had learned while working with Patty that her "hunches" were part of her super power as Front Desk Girl. It was her ability to foresee problems for guests in hotels before they actually happened. I never doubted her hunches, and they had always been right so far.

I banged on the door, then rang the doorbell. We both stepped back, trying to get away from the smell a little and waited.

Nothing.

I banged on the door again, then shouted, "Bookkeeper, it's Poker Boy. I need to talk to you!"

Nothing.

The super ability that kept me out of bad situations and bad poker hands was going off like a large gong in my head. Something was very wrong here, and my warning wanted me to avoid it. I often ignored that warning, especially in rescue situations.

I glanced at Patty. "You feeling it?"

She nodded.

Suddenly, a car pulled up behind Patty's car and Screamer climbed out. There was no reason for him to be here except to warn us about something or tell us that Laverne had been found. I was hoping for the latter, but my senses were telling me that wasn't the case.

We went down the driveway to meet him, trying to put some distance between us and the smell radiating out of that house.

"Glad I caught you," Screamer said. "You could be walking into a trap. It's The Bookkeeper who has had a problem with Lady Luck lately."

"You're kidding," I said. "He's no more than a superhero like we are. Why would he go up against Lady Luck herself?"

"He's crazy," Patty said, waving her hand in front of her nose to make her point, as if any of us could forget the smell The Bookkeeper lived in.

"He's been claiming that he can prove that luck is not needed in the universe," Screamer said, "that it is a man-made assumption to explain statistical occurrences."

"If he actually proved that, then Lady Luck would vanish," Patty said.

"And The Bookkeeper would be in charge," I said, glancing at the dark, ugly, smelling house behind us. "We need to get in there and find out what is really going on."

I went back to Patty's car and got my hat and coat and put them on. Smell or not, I was going to need the power. Patty grabbed a flashlight out of her glove box, then the three of us headed up the driveway toward the front door, fighting our way into the waves of smell.

At the front door, Patty put her hand on the door handle and I could hear the lock click.

The super ability that kept me out of bad situations and bad poker hands was going off like a large gong in my head.

It seemed that another power that Front Desk Girl had was helping people into their rooms after they'd locked themselves out. I just figured that power would be in making a new key, but I had learned a few cases back that it extended to opening just about anything that was locked.

"I'm going to be ready to shift us out of time," I said as I took Patty's hand. "Screamer, stay close."

He nodded. I had discovered during the problems with the Ghost Slots that an extension of my ability to stop and analyze a poker hand extended to taking myself out of time, or basically freezing time around me. Stan had first showed me that trick, but it wasn't until I was with Patty that I had learned how to do it myself.

On our last adventure, I had saved the three of us from getting killed by a huge wall of water washing down a dry gulch as we looked for an ancient burial ground of the Silicon Suckers. I just stopped time and the three of us moved out of the way of the water.

I just hoped that if something happened here I could do it again quickly.

It was just too bad that none of the three of us had an odor-repelling super power.

I led the way as we waded into the thick smell of the dark living room. The air got warmer, which made the smell even worse, if that was possible. The farther we got into the room, the more worried about this I felt.

The living room was piled high with rotting boxes of who-knew-what kind of trash. A path wound its way through the boxes toward the hallway and the back room where The Bookkeeper kept his computer set up with a small bed tucked in one corner.

In the faint light of the flashlight that Patty held, I could see littered remains of hundreds of different meals, mostly T.V. dinners, some still covered with black flies. Disgusting didn't begin to describe it.

Behind me Patty coughed softly and Screamer just said "Oh, man."

The house was a standard ranch house, with three bedrooms and a bath down a hallway off the living room. I knew, from the last time I had been here, that The Bookkeeper had set up his computer in the first bedroom on the right, across from a bathroom that smelled like the toilet had been used and used and not flushed in five years.

A faint light came from the computer room, and the humming sounds of powerful computers working filled the hallway.

Every sense in my body was telling me to turn and get out of here, to lay down this hand and just go to the next one. But sometimes in a hand you are what is called "pot committed," and in this instance, we were committed to finding out what was happening in that small bedroom, no matter how much I really didn't want to know.

I eased into the room where The Bookkeeper sat hunched over a keyboard, his fingers flying faster over the keys than I thought humanly possible.

"Bookkeeper," I said. "It's Poker Boy."

"I was wrong," he said, not stopping. "I'm sure I was wrong. I just have to prove it."

"Wrong about what?" I asked, stepping far enough into the small room that Patty and Screamer could move into the door behind me. In my mind I extended an area around the three of us and held that image just in case I needed to shift us out of time very, very quickly. I had no idea what The Bookkeeper would do next, but I wanted to be ready for anything.

"About luck," he said. "I have to prove she exists very quickly, before everything starts to unravel."

He pointed to his right between keystrokes; then, without missing a beat, kept typing.

"Oh, my," Patty said from behind me, flashing her light to the right where The Bookkeeper had pointed. In the beam of light, unseen in the darkness of the room, was Lady Luck. Actually, it was just a faint, shimmering image of Lady Luck, frozen in mid-sentence. The beam from Patty's flashlight went right through her.

Even like that, Lady Luck still scared hell out of me.

"She's slowly vanishing," Screamer said.

FOUR

"I USED TWELVE of the world's most powerful computers, linked up, to prove that luck did not exist," The Bookkeeper said, never looking up, never stopping his work. "And she ended up here, frozen in a moment, slowly fading. I had no intention of killing Lady Luck. I was just trying to prove a point."

"And if she vanishes completely?" Patty asked.

"Then slowly the rest of the world starts to do the same. Everything as we know it will slowly unravel."

"Why?" I asked.

"I don't know," The Bookkeeper said. "But that's what the computers tell me will happen if Luck dies."

"And now you're trying to do what exactly?" I asked.

"Prove that luck, Lady Luck does exist," he said.

I glanced back at Patty and Screamer. Patty's wonderful eyes were wider than normal which let me know she was both afraid and very worried. Screamer just looked intent, staring at Lady Luck.

Prove that luck existed. How could anyone do that?

I concentrated for an instant and took all three of us out of time, leaving The Bookkeeper in mid-stoke of the keyboard. We needed to talk and not have him hear us. I could hold all three of us in a bubble out of time for about a minute.

"Do you actually think The Bookkeeper's calculations brought Laverne here?" Patty asked.

"I have no doubt of that," Screamer said.

"Neither do I," I said. "Statistics are one of the greatest forces in the world, governing everything in every detail of life as we know it. I'm sure that power could do this, especially to Lady Luck, and she wouldn't even know what hit her. I've seen it a million times in poker hand after poker hand. Statistics win out over luck."

"I agree," Screamer said. "And clearly The Bookkeeper here is a master of statistics."

"And now he's trying to undo what he has done," Patty said.

I started to agree, but then one of my special powers kicked in. It was a power that sort of had a faint "ding" that signaled to my mind that it was in use. A "ding" that I had missed something that was important to the situation. When I heard that "ding" in my mind, I always stopped and went back over what had just happened. The power had saved me a lot of money on the poker tables.

It took me a moment, because I was also holding the bubble of the three of us out of time, but then I realized what I had missed. The Bookkeeper was not in charge of statistics, was not the master of them at all. He was only a lowly superhero like we were. He had a boss just like the rest of us.

I dropped us back to real time. "Bookkeeper, who is your boss?"

"A guy named Harold. Haven't seen him in a few hundred years."

"We'll be right back," I said, then nodded to Screamer and Patty that we should head outside.

The Bookkeeper didn't even slow down in the slightest.

The moment we were back outside into the warm Christmas Eve night, I shouted into the air, "Stan!"

He appeared near Patty's car and then motioned for us to stop about five feet away, wrinkling his nose. "Wow, do you three smell. What do you need?"

"Who is Harold? And who is Harold's boss?"

Stan frowned. "Harold is the God of Mathematics. He and the God of Physics, Merle, and the God of Chemistry, Bettie, hang around together and pretty much look down their noses at all the Gambling Gods and even the other science gods. They pretty much run their own area. I don't know if they actually report in to anyone these days. Why?"

"We found Laverne," I said, nodding to the dark house. "Is there any bad blood between them and Laverne?"

"You found her!" Stan said.

"Hang on," I said, stopping Stan from rushing into the house. "We don't really know what's going on yet and I think we had better find out before doing anything. So any bad blood between Laverne and any of the science gods?"

Stan shook his head, "None that I know of."

A moment later a heavy-set man wearing a three-piece suit appeared beside Stan. He had an unlit cigar in one hand. He glanced around and then wrinkled his nose. "The Bookkeeper's place I assume?"

Stan nodded.

Patty, Screamer, and I said nothing. It wasn't often that the god who was second in command to Laverne just appeared in front of you. Burt scared me, but not half as bad as Laverne did.

"Any fights lately between Laverne and the science geeks?" Stan asked.

"Nothing that I know of," Burt said. "Why?"

"Then we need them here," I said, "and maybe the god in charge of humanities or human nature as well."

Burt stared at me like I was a fly on a steak he was about to eat. I stood my ground, even though every sense in my body wanted me to just cower away.

"Why?" he demanded.

I quickly told him what we had found in there, and what The Bookkeeper had done and was now trying to undo. I finished with "He needs help, and it isn't the kind of help any of us can give him. In fact, if we try anything, we might end up completely killing Laverne."

"Poker Boy is right," Screamer said. "The Bookkeeper might be able to prove that luck doesn't exist, but proving luck exists is another matter."

I couldn't have said it better myself, so I said nothing more.

Burt stared at Screamer, then at me, then at Patty. A moment later we were all standing in a very large, very plush library office, with books that went up all four walls to a very high ceiling. As far as I could see in all directions, it was library walls and books. There had to be millions of books in here. Just the thought of that gave me a headache. I got a lot of headaches back in my college days.

A crackling fire filled a large stone fireplace on one wall, and three over-stuffed leather chairs circled the fireplace. Clearly this was where Harold, Merle, and Bettie spent a lot of time.

At the moment all three were standing, as if informed we were coming.

"What do we owe this Christmas Eve visit to?" asked a man with a heavy cardigan sweater and an unlit pipe in his hand. Another man with thick round glasses and a bald head stood beside him, and Bettie stood slightly off to one side looking the perfect image of an old school teacher from the Wild West.

"Thank you for seeing us, Harold," Burt said.

"What is that odor?" Bettie said, waving her hand in front of her nose. Then the God of Chemistry waved her hand at me and Screamer and Patty and the foul stench of The Bookkeeper's house vanished.

I wanted to thank her, but instead kept silent as Burt quickly explained what one of their lowly superheroes had done to Lady Luck.

"The Bookkeeper did that?" Harold said, smiling to himself. "I am impressed."

"That explains the smell," Bettie said, nodding to us. "You went to see him, didn't you?"

"It would be impressive," Burt said, "Except that Laverne is trapped by his equations, and slowly fading from existence."

"And The Bookkeeper is working as fast as he can to prove that luck *does* exist to bring her back," I said. "But he needs help."

Harold smiled and nodded. "I can imagine he would at that. He would make the equations far, far harder than they would need to be."

Merle nodded. "It's like a quantum physics problem, actually. The Bookkeeper might have been able to prove that, in perfect conditions, statistics prove that luck does not exist. That would have been enough to trap Laverne without warning. But luck is governed and influenced by the observer. And thus the observer changes the equation by simply observing it. Simple, actually."

I didn't think it was so simple, but clearly Harold and Bettie understood him. Burt, Stan, and the three of us were just nodding, as if we actually understood any of that.

"Can you help The Bookkeeper reverse what he has done to Laverne?" Burt asked.

Harold nodded and turned to me and Patty and Screamer. "Since the three of you have been in that house once tonight, I assume you can go back in. Correct?"

We all nodded.

"Tell The Bookkeeper I told him to add into his equation the factor of an observer. That should break what is holding Laverne. But tell him to go slowly. Very slowly."

Burt nodded. "Thanks. I'm sure Laverne will stop by to thank you as well."

FIVE

AN INSTANT LATER we were back out in front of The Bookkeeper's home.

I glanced at Stan and Burt, then turned to Patty and Screamer. "No need for the two of you to go in there again."

The moment I said that, I knew that I was wrong.

Patty shook her head and Screamer looked worried.

"I think we all need to do this," Patty said.

Burt and Stan both nodded. "Harold told all three of you to do it, so it's going to take the three of you for some strange reason.

I couldn't argue with my two bosses, and my little voice, the one that controlled most of my actions, both at a poker table and away from it, was now happy again.

Bracing ourselves once more against the smell, which is just damned impossible to do, we fought our way upstream through the front room and back to where The Bookkeeper pounded the keys.

Laverne looked very, very faint.

My little voice told me that I needed to get us all close together and be ready to get us out of real time very quickly. Harold had said that what I was to tell The Bookkeeper would break the equations holding Laverne. I didn't like the sounds of the word "break" at all.

"Bookkeeper," I said when Screamer and Patty were in position beside me, "we went to see Harold."

The Bookkeeper just kept working, his fingers pounding the keyboard, the screens in front of him flashing numbers and calculations faster than I could follow, even if I knew what I was looking at.

"Harold said to add in the factor of an observer into your equation."

"Sure he did, sure," The Bookkeeper said.

Laverne seemed to fade a little more and The Bookkeeper just kept working.

I clicked us out of time and turned to Screamer. "He doesn't believe me, he's so trapped and scared."

"I can show him the image of Harold and Merle and Bettie," Screamer said.

"Patty, can you calm him down?" I asked. I knew that another of Patty's special abilities is to get a person to calm down when they are very, very upset.

"I can," Patty said. She looked worried still.

"What are you thinking?" I asked, staring as best I could in the dim light into her dark brown eyes.

"I'm worried about what's going to happen when the spell holding one of the most powerful women in all of time breaks."

"Yeah, me too," I said. "And I don't think The Bookkeeper, to rescue Laverne, can go slowly. I don't think there's enough time."

Screamer nodded that he too had thought about that.

Patty looked at me. "If he can't do it slowly, you need to surround The Bookkeeper as well the moment he types in the equation that will break the hold on Laverne."

I nodded. "The timing on this is going to be critical. Screamer, you be touching The Bookkeeper and Patty and I will be touching you, so we know the instant we need to move."

"Got it," he said.

I wanted to take a deep breath and say, "Let's do it." But a deep breath of this air might knock me out, so instead I just nodded and released us back into real time.

As a unit we stepped over behind The Bookkeeper. I held Patty's hand and then touched Screamer's shoulder, keeping my mind focused on an area around the four of us.

When Patty touched Screamer an instant later, I got a sense of her thoughts, her worries. They were the same as mine. And Screamer's. We were all scared to death.

Screamer reached forward and touched the back of The Bookkeeper's shoulder. All I could feel at that point was massive panic and fear.

Patty quickly calmed him down, and me and Screamer as well with a simple thought.

"I see, I see, I understand," The Bookkeeper said, nodding as Screamer transferred the images from the vast library into his head.

"But I can't go slowly."

He stopped and turned to us, but because we were all touching Screamer, we all knew exactly what he meant. Laverne was too far gone. Going slowly was not an option, and we all knew it because we were all linked.

So Screamer put in The Bookkeeper's head what we planned on doing, and The Bookkeeper nodded. "Only chance we have."

He turned back to his keyboard, paused only for a second, then began quickly typing again.

In the corner Laverne started to firm up, slowly, her image not so faint.

The Bookkeeper kept pounding the keys.

Patty kept us all calm.

Screamer kept the communication links opened.

And I stood ready to snap us out of time and away from any danger.

"That should do it," The Bookkeeper said, pounding one finger on the enter key.

Now!

The thought from Screamer was like a shout in my head.

I snapped us out of time a tiny fraction of a second before the explosion started to tear through the house and all space around us.

Close. Too damned close.

Screamer grabbed The Bookkeeper and yanked his small frame out of the chair, carrying him as we all turned for the door.

"Stay near me," I said, working to hold the bubble around all four of us as we worked our way toward the front door. Patty kept her hand in mine, sending as much strength and energy into me as she could to help me hold the field as long as I could.

Outside, on the driveway, Stan and Burt were standing frozen, clearly waiting for us to come out, not realizing I had taken us out of time. The four of us moved down the driveway toward them, and I surrounded them as well with my field, barely holding it.

"Stan," I said, the moment he and Burt were inside the bubble and could see us, "I need help holding this time bubble."

Instantly Stan took over and I almost slumped to the ground with the release. I was still creating the bubble, but Stan was powering it.

"I have a hunch we need to be a little farther away than this," Screamer said.

"I agree," The Bookkeeper said, his breath worse than the smell of his house.

"No need to worry," Burt said. "Stan can you hold this for another few seconds?"

"No problem," Stan said.

Burt closed his eyes and focused for a moment, then nodded and opened them.

"It's been a while since I needed to do that."

"What?" Patty asked.

"I put a force field cone around the house, so that any explosion will be focused upward about five hundred feet. We're outside that cone, so it's safe to let us go."

Stan nodded to me and I released us all back into real time.

The explosion was deafening as The Bookkeeper's house just flat vanished into a dust cloud that went straight up.

A very smelly dust cloud. The neighbors, and much of Las Vegas, were not going to be happy with that smell.

Out of the dust cloud and force field that Burt had raised walked Laverne. She was totally nude, since the explosion had vaporized her clothes. And she looked really pissed off.

"Someone want to explain to me just what the hell is going on?"

Burt sort of pointed at Laverne's midsection and at that moment Laverne

noticed she was nude. I had to admit, for such an ancient god, she kept in pretty good shape.

Clothes appeared on her and she didn't blink, keeping her stare on Burt. Clearly they were communicating in a way I didn't want to think about.

After a moment, she turned on The Bookkeeper. But before she could do anything to him, Harold appeared beside the smelly man and nodded. "Glad to see you well, Laverne. I'll take care of The Bookkeeper. Very sorry for the bother."

And then they were gone.

Laverne took a deep breath, then coughed. Into the air she shouted "Bettie, can you do something about this smell?"

A moment later the air around us smelled like a spring meadow. Even my jacket and hat smelled like a freshly mown lawn.

Up and down the street people were coming out to stare at the giant hole where The Bookkeeper's house used to be. No doubt, the property values in the neighborhood had just taken a huge jump, but I was going to be real curious to know how the police explained this one to the press.

Laverne turned to the three of us, and stared first at me.

I wanted to melt right there into the driveway, but instead stood my ground and stared back at her, giving her my best poker face. I couldn't talk, but I could stare just fine.

"It seems," she said after a very, very long moment, "that I once again owe you three a thank you."

"It's just our job," Patty said, smiling.

"Well," Laverne said, "thank you for doing your job so well, and for saving me. I hope you have a great holiday. You all three deserve some time off."

With that, she and Burt vanished.

Stan turned to us and just smiled. "Nice job, guys." Then he too vanished.

Screamer clapped his hands together and laughed. "Damned if we didn't do it again."

I was still too stunned to say anything. Seems face-to-face meetings with Lady Luck just did that to me.

"There's a large steak waiting for me down at the MGM Grand," Screamer said. "You two want to join me?"

Patty put her arm around my waist and smiled. "I think we'll take a rain check on that."

Two hours later, after a long, long shower with far too much use of soap between us, and a long, wonderful time in bed, I stared at the beautiful women lying next to me.

"What are you thinking?" she asked.

I just leaned in and kissed her as a response.

Right at that moment all was well in the world. There was no doubt that luck still existed.

And that I was the luckiest man alive.

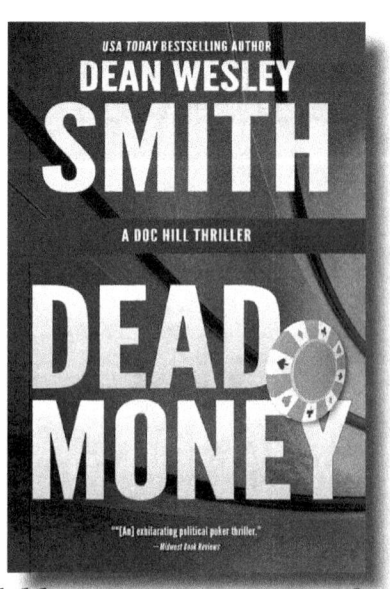

Available at Your Favorite Bookstore

Now Available
from all your favorite booksellers
in trade paper and electronic editions.

USA TODAY BESTSELLING AUTHOR

DEAN WESLEY SMITH

THE HIGH EDGE

A SEEDERS UNIVERSE NOVEL

Dean Wesley **Smith**

USA Today Bestselling Writer

WHAT
WOULD YOU DO?

PETER
THE HERMIT

The world destroyed by an asteroid in five days?

What would you do? We all like to think we wouldn't act like Peter. Or maybe we would.

A close-up look at the end of the world. Maybe.

PETER THE HERMIT

ONE

THE APARTMENT SMELLED like stale socks, soured milk, and pee. More pee than soured milk, but the combination of the odors was starting to get through Peter's drunken state and make the beer taste funny. Ruining the taste of a good beer was a crime against nature, especially if the beer was the best he could find down at the corner Circle K an hour after they had announced the asteroid was going to hit Earth and destroy all life.

Actually, he had managed to get the last five cases of the good stuff, and with the power off the last two days had grown to enjoy it warm.

He finished off the can with a deep gulp, and without looking tossed the dead soldier in the general direction of the overflowing trashcan he had put as a target in the corner of the living room. Then he turned to see if his shot found its mark.

The can bounced once off the wall spraying beer on the console big-screen television next to the garbage can, clanged against some soup cans he'd put on top of the pile of trash at some point earlier in the day, and then bounced back toward him across the floor.

It came to rest halfway across his wood dining room floor against another beer can he'd tossed yesterday.

Damn! One of his worst shots. And they said practice made perfect. Well, it looked as if he needed more practice.

And that meant he needed another beer.

He pushed himself up out of the brown leather armchair and scratched his nuts. The T-shirt and loose boxer shorts he'd been wearing for two days stuck to him like his first wife, clinging and itching. He pulled them away from his skin, just like he'd done with her. He was glad both she and his second wife were gone. Good riddance to both of them.

He was sweating harder now than he had in days. Too bad he couldn't open a few windows and cool this place down a little, and get rid of some of the smell. But he didn't dare even open his blinds at this point. Too damn dangerous.

Besides, he didn't want that world out there coming into his life any more than it already was. He was finished with that world.

His comb-over hung down beside his head, and his whiskers were headed toward a new beard. Yesterday, or maybe the day before, he had broken the mirrors in the bathroom and on his closet door so that he would never have to look at himself again.

Peter yawned, sticking out his gut like it was a prize to show the world, unlike the old days when he used to hide it under expensive suits and work in the gym at tightening his stomach.

Now that all seemed so damned stupid.

He turned and headed for the bathroom, the dim light through the blinds making the apartment seem like it was out of focus and in black and white. At least when he was drinking beer he got exercise standing and going to the bathroom. Why hadn't he thought of that before the "big day of doom" was announced?

Five minutes later he was back in his chair, an opened can of Campbell's Pork and Beans in one hand, a beer in the other. It had taken him a good three of those minutes figuring out how to use the old manual can opener. He managed it fine when sober, but that thing always became the puzzle of the ages after ten or fifteen beers.

From outside he heard a loud bang, more than likely a gunshot, and then a scream. *A woman's scream.* What the hell was a woman doing out on the street? Stupid, really stupid.

Then another two shots and the sounds died away, leaving him to peacefully enjoy his beer and beans.

He alternated on the cans.

A gulp of beer.

A big spoonful of beans.

Another gulp of beer.

The beer won the race and the can lofted at the overflowing trash can. Again his shot was high, but this time the can spun and hit the television. Ten days ago hitting the big screen with an empty beer can would have been unthinkable. Now he counted that as an extra point.

Two more mouthfuls of beans and that can and spoon headed in the same direction. The can actually stayed on top of the pile.

Three points.

The spoon ended up behind the decorative drapes over the window on the other side of the room. A streak of brown beans dripped down the wall beside the television like blood.

He shook his head and stood, heading for the kitchen for another beer. These days everything looked like blood. And the only way he was going to ever escape those thoughts was just keep drinking.

This time he took the entire case of beer and put it beside his chair before sitting back down. Screw the exercise. He hadn't needed it when he worked his old corporate job, he didn't need it now.

Screw what his second wife had said.

Screw what the insurance man had said.

Screw what his doctors had said. They were all going to die at the same time he did, if they weren't already dead from the riots and fires. He wasn't going to live any longer just because he had exercised for years.

He drank most of a beer in one gulp and tossed the can, watching it roll to a stop on the wood floor as he grabbed another.

Screw them all, and the stupid world as well. He, Peter Danials, just didn't give a rat's ass any more.

Five, maybe six beers later, he drifted off.

Or passed out.

TWO

THE NEXT THING he knew more shots were echoing through the streets outside, it was pitch dark in the apartment, and his bladder was about to explode.

He stumbled through the apartment to the bathroom, aimed in the general direction of the full toilet, and then leaned against the wall, his eyes closed, pretending everything was fine as he relieved himself.

He could still feel the beer buzz, but not enough to dull the ache and the fear of dying, or the smell of the toilet that hadn't been flushed in days. Outside, from all the shouting and gunshots, it sounded like some of the riots had moved closer to his apartment. God only knew what people were fighting about now. To him there just didn't seem to be much point.

Why didn't they all just find some beer, have a party, screw each other into peaceful sleep, and then get up and do it all over again until things ended? Nope, not the idiots who called themselves humans. Instead they were fighting and killing each other and just being stupid.

Well screw all of them. He had his beer, his apartment, the rest of his short life. He didn't need anyone else.

He finished peeing, bean-farted twice, and then felt his way out of the bathroom and toward the kitchen.

After days and days of having the power gone, he'd gotten pretty good at not kicking anything in the dark. He had matches, a few candles, and a slowly dying flashlight, but there just didn't seem to be much need to turn them on.

Outside the fighting slowly moved into the distance, leaving the night in the city dead quiet. He felt around the counter knocking over empty cans and dirty dishes until he found the last case of beer. Maybe now, before he started drinking again, he should try to make his way out to find some more supplies.

Or maybe he should just give it up, drink the last of the beer, eat the last of his food, and then find his pistol and put a shot through the roof of his mouth.

Or maybe, better still, take the beer to the roof, drink it all, and then stumble over the edge. That wouldn't be as quick as the gun, but good enough.

Decisions, decisions. What was a man to do?

His last wife had always said that he made decisions without enough facts. Maybe that was true. She had decided to leave him when the "big day of doom" was announced. Why, he would now never know. She had simply packed a few clothes and walked away without a word. It seemed she didn't want to drink away her last five days of life.

Well screw her. She didn't know what she was missing.

So now how much time did he have left anyway? He'd lost track of what day it even was. He needed facts to figure out what path to take.

In the pitch darkness of his kitchen he found the flashlight right where he'd left it on the windowsill over the sink. Usually that window looked out on the open courtyard in the middle of his apartment building. He and his wife had always kept it open, letting the breezes and city smells fill the apartment.

Now the window was locked closed and the blinds were tightly drawn. But even with the blinds drawn, he turned his back on the window and huddled over the light as he turned it on.

The beam was amazingly bright, making him blink as his eyes adjusted.

Then, cupping the light so no one might see it through the blinds, he turned and looked at the calendar on the wall. October fifteenth was crossed out in red and he had scribbled over the page the words "End of the World."

He turned and quickly found his expensive watch where he had put it on top of the refrigerator. The watch was still running, and the little calendar said it was October thirteenth.

Two more days to live.

Damn! He didn't have enough beer for two more days.

He was either going to have to end it soon, or he was going to have to break out the bottles of vodka and gin he kept for guests if he wanted to be drunk when the big rock came powering in two days from now.

Maybe the gun wasn't a bad idea after all. He drank vodka, but he didn't like it as much as beer. Warm beer or warm vodka, he'd take the beer every day. But he doubted there was any beer left anywhere close by that he might be able to loot.

He took a beer from his last case, opened it, and took a long warm drink. This was a decision that would take a few beers to figure out.

THREE

HE TURNED and started back toward the living room, taking the flashlight with him.

Suddenly, two steps from his chair, every light in the apartment came on, then the television blared into life.

"What the…."

He stared at the big screen television as the cameras panned what seemed like millions of people dancing and cheering in the streets of some city.

Then the announcer came on, clearly dirty and unshaven, but smiling like Peter had never seen anyone smile.

"For those of you who are just getting power back," the announcer said, "we can report that the asteroid is going to miss Earth. This is not just false hope, people. This is real. The asteroid will barely graze through the planet's high atmosphere in two days, but will not be pulled into a full

Now Available
from all your favorite booksellers
in trade paper and electronic editions.

collision. Scientists have been working on new computer models and there is no doubt we will all survive this."

At this point the announcer went on into details about what had happened, what caused the change,—or better put, the *mistake*—of a few hundreds of miles in calculating the asteroid's path.

That mistake had caused the entire world to think it was going to end.

How many people had died because of that mistake?

Peter stopped listening and dropped down into his lounge chair, the empty beer can still in his hand. One minute he was going to die, the next he was going to live.

Everyone was going to live.

That was something that took some time to sink in, just as the news of the asteroid collision had taken time to sink in when announced.

He sat there watching the pictures of the people dancing in the streets.

An hour, maybe two. He didn't pay any attention. It just wasn't sinking in.

Then slowly, outside his closed windows, he started hearing cheering and shouting and loud crying.

He looked around his garbage-filled apartment, then stood and moved over to the window. At first he peeked out cautiously; then, when he saw the people hugging and dancing and pouring out of the buildings, he opened the window wide and took a deep breath of the fresh air.

Unbelievable, simply unbelievable, just like the news of the end of the world had been.

Now the world was saved.

Now things would continue. Maybe not the same, but they would continue.

He watched the crowds for a few minutes, maybe longer, then went back and stood in front of his television watching the images coming in of celebration after celebration around the world.

It was real.

It was real, of that there was no doubt.

The world was going to live.

He moved back to the window to watch the crowd again, letting the news sink in finally

Then he turned and looked at his apartment.

It was a mess, and so was he.

So was the entire world, but things could be cleaned up. It would take time, but it was possible.

He went to the bathroom and flushed the toilet without looking at it, then moved back into the kitchen and opened up the window to try to clear some of the smell of rotted food and dead beer.

Glancing around, he nodded to himself and pulled out a black garbage bag, and moved into the living room to try to take back, and try to forget, the last three days of his life.

That too would take time, but it was possible if he moved slowly.

One empty beer can at a time.

USA TODAY BESTSELLING AUTHOR

DEAN WESLEY SMITH

AN EASY SHOT

A GOLF THRILLER

In the first installments, Seattle Police Detectives Bonnie and Craig, while taking a late night walk on a Scottsdale Arizona golf course, happen to overhear a conversation between two men plotting to kill a United States Senator.

At the same time, a young golf professional's wife is kidnapped. Scheduled to play with the Senator, he must do what they ask or his wife will die.

Bonnie and Craig get the FBI and local police involved. Everything is set and they play with the Senator to help protect him.

Nothing goes wrong, but that night, they see the two men again who they had overheard.

Now, the next morning, starting the second round of golf, everyone waits and watches.

A horrific accident on the golf course almost kills the Senator, but he is fine and sent on to Washington while they set a trap for the man coming to kill Danny, the young golf professional.

The man is killed in the hotel room by Craig and an FBI agent.

Danny's wife is rescued and at that point Bonnie and Craig think they can now go back to their vacation. Nope.

They are kidnapped and locked in a closet of the home of the man who tried to kill the Senator.

AN EASY SHOT

Part 8 of 8

CHAPTER TWENTY-FIVE

Monday, April 10th
3:10 a.m.

MAXWELL LOOKED at the rumpled and very tired Hagar as he staggered into the police station. A couple other night-shift detectives laughed, but no one said anything.

"This had better be damned good," Hagar said. "I was dreaming about swimming naked with a dozen women when you so rudely woke me up."

Maxwell laughed. "No wonder you look so tired." He pointed at the screen of a monitor sitting on a desk and punched play. He had watched these images a dozen times over the last ten minutes and still couldn't figure out exactly what they meant.

Hagar frowned. The image showed a tall wall and some people coming down the street toward the camera.

"The Robins estate," Maxwell said. "Filmed less than an hour ago."

"I know where it's at," Hagar said, "but who are the people?"

"Wait," Maxwell said.

On screen the images of the people became clearer and clearer.

"Holy shit, you're kidding?"

"I'm not," Maxwell said. "That's Bonnie and Craig, their hands tied, being led into the Robins estate by two of Robins' goons. I checked their room and they are not there."

"Robins kidnapped them?" Hagar almost shouted as the film showed Bonnie and Craig being walked right through the front gate. "Why the hell would he do that?"

"I don't know the answer to that question," Maxwell said, "but they haven't come out of there yet."

Hagar shook his head. "Didn't they know your van was there filming everything?"

"I guess not," Maxwell said. "Or I doubt they would have taken them in this way."

Hagar glanced at Maxwell. "Are you thinking what I think you are thinking? You want to go in after them?"

Maxwell nodded. "I've got agents flying up here from Tucson and down from Vegas. I can have a force of over thirty men ready to roll in forty minutes."

"And you think Bonnie and Craig are still alive in there?" Hagar asked.

"At the moment I do," Maxwell said, "but the longer we wait, the less chance I give them. And I give them no chance when Robins discovers they helped trick him with the Senator."

"Damn, you're right," Hagar said. He rewound the film again quickly and watched them walk past the truck and through the main gate.

To Maxwell there was no doubt both Craig and Bonnie were tied and being led at gunpoint.

"Robins might have over fifty men in there," Hagar said, "and from what I've observed about those men, they aren't afraid to defend that place."

"I assumed as much," Maxwell said. "That's why we need to work together on this."

Hagar just stared at him for a moment, then said, "You're nuts, you know that?"

Maxwell nodded.

"Shit, shit, shit!" Hagar said, turning from Maxwell and picking up the phone.

Ten minutes later Hagar had permission to work with the FBI from the Chief of Police.

Thirty minutes later Hagar had a force of over fifty men, including a SWAT team from Phoenix, staged at different locations around the Robins estate, armed and ready to go when the order was given.

Maxwell knew that if this turned into a gunfight, it was going to go down poorly. Their best bet was to try to talk their way in and disarm guards as they went.

Hagar was convinced that there was going to be no talking their way inside those walls. He had calls out for even more help to stand ready. He told Maxwell that if this didn't turn out to be the Alamo west, he'd be surprised.

That was the last thing Maxwell wanted to have happen. But inside those walls were two kidnapped cops and a man they suspected of trying to kill a United States Senator. He had no other choice.

They had to go in.

CHAPTER TWENTY-SIX

Monday, April 10th
4:03 a.m.

BONNIE HAD DOZED lightly for most of the past half hour, and Craig had let her. The closet had gotten cold and Bonnie had pulled down one of the expensive wool coats that hung in there to use as a cover. And she was using Craig as a pillow, something he didn't mind at all.

Craig had talked her into closing her eyes for a short time. There was just no point in both of them trying to stay alert. There wasn't much they could do until Robins decided to let them out. Unless they wanted to take a chance on getting shot trying to escape, and at the moment Craig didn't much like that idea.

So until something happened, they sat on the floor, in the dark, and waited.

Craig guessed that at least an hour or more had gone by since Robins had tossed them into the closet. And if that was the case, they were getting closer and closer to the Senator's press conference in Washington. Craig had no desire to still be Robins' prisoner when he discovered the Senator was still healthy and voting.

A slight snoring noise rumbled the closet and Craig eased Bonnie sideways. Usually she didn't snore, but considering how tired she was, and the circumstances, it was understandable.

Bonnie mumbled and cuddled against his side as the snoring sound happened again. He shook her lightly, then when her eyes popped open he whispered, "Shhh, listen."

The snoring sound came again.

She sat upright in the darkness, then leaned toward him and whispered, "The guard's asleep."

"That's what I thought," Craig said.

"Think we can break that lock open?" she asked, her voice barely audible.

"Yeah," he said, silently standing and moving his legs to make sure the circulation hadn't left them. He had taken out other locks much stronger than the one on this closet door. And from the sounds of the snoring, the guard was leaning against the door. So the break-out would have to be strong enough to snap the lock and shove the guard aside at the same time. If the wood in the door held, it would work.

"What do you want me to do?" Bonnie asked.

"Be ready to hit the guy on the head with one of those wooden hangers," Craig whispered.

The snoring stopped for an instant, the guy shifted against the door, moving more away from the lock, then a moment later the snoring started again.

Craig let out the breath he had been holding. "Ready?"

"As I'll ever be," Bonnie whispered.

Craig braced himself against the back wall of the closet. It was just a little too far from the door to give him the best force on his kick. He used both hands to lightly pull on the hanger bar. It seemed very solid and secure in place. It would hold his weight long enough for him to kick the door open, he was sure.

He leaned toward Bonnie and whispered, "Here we go."

"Careful," she whispered back.

"You too," he said.

He put himself in position directly behind the door's handle, then with two deep breaths, he pulled himself up on the bar and with all the force he could manage in both legs, kicked the door with both feet.

It smashed open like it hadn't even been latched.

Bonnie was through the door before he could even let go of the bar.

The guard had been shoved head over heels away from the door by the force of Craig's kicks.

Bonnie was around the open door and over the guard by the time the guy even started to get up. One very hard smack against the side of the head with the wooden hanger and the guy went back to sleep.

"He's going to have one massive headache when he wakes up," Bonnie said, smiling at her husband.

"Remind me to never get you mad at me."

Craig grabbed the guy's rifle, a semi-automatic with a dozen rounds in the clip. The guy had one in the chamber, ready to fire.

Bonnie dug around in the guard's pockets and pulled out two more clips for the rifle and a 44 caliber pistol with extra rounds. Then she took an earplug from the guard's ear and a small communications device from his front pocket of his vest.

She handed the communication equipment to Craig.

"Better find out what his name is," Craig said, "so we can answer a call to him."

Bonnie quickly flipped the guy over and dug his wallet out of his back pocket. She flipped it open and then snorted. "Dwight. His name is Dwight."

A security guard named Dwight. No wonder he had fallen asleep.

She stuck the wallet back in the guy's pants and stood.

"Keep watch," he said.

He grabbed the guard and pulled him back into the closet, then tied his hands and feet with the rope they had been tied with.

The closet door, with a little work, almost looked like nothing had happened to it by the time Craig got it closed again.

"Now what?" Bonnie asked.

Craig glanced down the corridor. There was a security camera trained on the corner about fifty feet away. And another one in the other direction down the hall. It looked like they were between them at least.

"There's got to be a major security system in this place, as well as at least twenty guards, if not a lot more," he said. He pointed at the cameras as he stuck the earplug in his ear.

"Damn," she said, "we move from here at all and they'll know we've escaped."

"So when we do move, we make the best of it," Craig said, "and move fast."

"Until then we wait here?" Bonnie asked.

In his ear Craig could hear the sudden excited talking of the front guards, as well as others along the perimeter of the estate. They were all reporting in that a large number of police had suddenly moved up into position.

"Exactly," he said, smiling at her. "But I don't think we're going to have to wait long. We're about to have the cavalry come to the rescue."

CHAPTER TWENTY-SEVEN

Monday, April 10th
4:27 a.m.

"ARE WE READY?" Maxwell asked Hagar.

"My people are," Hagar said, nodding as he listened to the last of status reports in his ear.

"So are mine," Maxwell said. "Let's do it."

Maxwell picked up a bullhorn as the two of them stepped around the police car and walked ten feet out into the middle of the road in front of the main gate of the Robins estate. Above them the stars were shining and the air was crisp and almost cold. Maxwell could see a dozen men in different positions inside the gate, guns all at rest. As long as they stayed that way, everything would be fine.

"Attention. This is the FBI," Maxwell shouted through the bullhorn, his voice echoing over the estate and into the rock hills behind it. "Open the gates and throw down your weapons. You are completely surrounded."

Nothing.

He knew that he had the horn set loud enough that anyone inside the buildings beyond those wall would be able to hear him as well. He would give good old Robins a moment to think about things, and then try again.

The silence of the late desert night seemed intense as Maxwell and Hagar waited. Inside the gate no one moved.

"This is the FBI!" Maxwell repeated through the horn. "Throw down your weapons and come out."

Again the silence seemed to crawl down over him like a giant bug trying to smother him. He could feel his own heart beating and the fear choking him. But he stood there, in the middle of the road, and waited for a response.

Then through the gate there was movement, but it took Maxwell a fraction of a second to realize it was the wrong kind of movement. One of the men just inside the gate to the right was raising his gun.

Another behind him was doing the same.

"Get down!" Hagar shouted and turned to get to cover.

Maxwell spun and ran, the ten steps between him and the shelter of the patrol car seemingly a thousand yards.

The air suddenly echoed with the sounds of gunfire. For an instant it was only a few shots, all coming from beyond the walls, then there was more and more until it was impossible to tell how many, as if strings of firecrackers were being shot off in a closed space.

Maxwell's agents were now returning fire, trying to cover him as he and Hagar got to shelter.

A bullet smashed into the car just beyond him.

Close!

Way too damned close!

He tried to dive for the shelter of the front fender of the car.

He didn't make it.

The burning feeling of the bullet cutting through the flesh of his back wasn't as bad as he expected. But the impact flipped him completely over, smashing him to the concrete. The fall hurt like hell, and he banged his head, knocking him into blackness for a moment.

He came to in time to feel Hagar's hands grab him and drag him beyond the car and over into a shallow ditch beside the road.

There was no pain.

That surprised him.

He just couldn't move.

That also surprised him.

He should feel pain, he should be able to move. It was as if the wind had been knocked out of him and all his energy taken.

"Damn!" Hagar said. "Officer down here!"

Two other men swarmed into the ditch beside him as the gun battle continued, the quiet of the night now a continuous roar of explosions.

Maxwell noted it all like watching it from a distance. For some reason he knew that things were not going well, but a part of him just no longer cared.

"Hang in there," Hagar yelled to him, but it was like the cop was shouting down a long tunnel.

Maxwell felt himself smile.

He had been shot and it hadn't really hurt.

And now he was going to die. He knew that as clearly as he had known anything in his life.

And that was all right as well.

This experience was not at all what he had expected death to feel like.

He looked up at the pained expression on Hagar's face and knew exactly what the cop wanted him to say.

How he knew, he wasn't sure, but he just knew.

He used one hand to pull Hagar down closer, then in his ear he said, "Get the damned son-of-a-bitch for me, would you?"

"I will," Hagar said.

Maxwell really didn't care, but he knew that Hagar did. And if the situation was reversed, Hagar would have said it for him as well.

Maxwell felt he was floating now, sort of watching what was happening to him like an observer from a distance. He was both in his body and watching them around his body.

There was no pain.

Just a wonderful sense of floating.

"Maxwell!"

The voice sort of pulled at him, but he ignored it. He liked the floating.

"Maxwell!" Hagar shouted. "Maxwell, stay with us!"

But Maxwell could see no point in staying.

And with that he died.

CHAPTER TWENTY-EIGHT

Monday, April 10th
4:32 a.m.

CRAIG WAS STUNNED when the shooting began.

"What the hell is going on?" Bonnie asked, clearly as afraid and as stunned as he was. They had both heard the faint demands of Maxwell as he told Robins' men to lay down their guns and come out. At the time the voice had cheered them.

Then in his ear Craig had heard the command come from Robins directly. "Keep the FBI out at all costs."

A moment later the shooting had started.

"The stupid ass ordered them to fight the FBI," Craig said, shaking his head in amazement. "What the hell is he thinking?"

"Maybe that's our problem," Bonnie said. "We keep expecting the man to think."

"Well, we need to stop this," Craig said. "There's a lot of good men out there getting fired on."

"And just two of us in here," Bonnie said. "You got any smart ideas?"

"Sure," Craig said. "We capture the head of this snake and tell him to shut things down."

Bonnie nodded and glanced down the hall. "I can remember how to get back to his study, but we're going to have to do it fast and without stopping."

"Agreed," Craig said. "I'll take the lead and you cover my back."

She pinched his butt. "I'll make sure this doesn't get shot off if you take care of that guy in front."

"Deal," he said.

Outside the gunfire was becoming even more intense. It was a war out there and unless it stopped quickly a lot of people were going to get hurt or killed.

He kissed her and then turned and headed down the hall, knowing she was right behind him.

At that moment what he really wanted was to lock them both in a closet and only come out when the shooting was over, but he knew neither one of them could do that.

They were cops. It was their lives.

And right now a lot of other cops were getting shot at. If they had the best chance of stopping it, they needed to take it.

They had to take it.

With the rifle leveled and ready to fire he went around the first corner under the camera. There was no one in the hallway.

He kept moving at a near run.

Bonnie stayed close behind, the sound of her footsteps almost matching his.

In about fifty paces the hallway opened up into a wide foyer with plants on one side and a door leading outside to the right.

The door into Robins' study was to the left and down another short hallway.

There was a guard poised, facing the exterior door, as if waiting for someone to come through.

Craig shouted, "Drop the gun!"

The guard was too stupid for words.

Instead of dropping the gun he spun and tried to fire.

Craig cut him down with a short blast, almost ripping the guard in half with the tight pattern of his bullets.

"To the left!" Bonnie said behind him and Craig headed that way.

Ahead of him a guard poked his head out of a door and Craig fired through the edge of the door and wood of the wall, aiming at where the man's midsection would be.

The guy jerked and fell out into the hallway, clearly dead. Any good cop knew that the wood and plasterboard of regular house walls didn't stop most bullets. This guy clearly had watched too much television thinking he was safe behind that door.

"Grab his rifle," Craig said as he checked the room the guard had been in for anyone else, and then moved on down the hall.

Robins' study was two more doors away.

Bonnie grabbed the rifle and kept guard behind him as Craig stared at that office door.

There was no doubt that there was someone on the other side of it waiting for him to come through.

And the minute he did, he was dead.

He didn't want to be dead just yet.

But there was a guy here that already had that distinction, and wouldn't mind a few more holes, Craig figured.

Craig went back and picked up the guy he had just killed, keeping the rifle in one hand as he did it. The dead guy wasn't that heavy, or the adrenaline in Craig's body was working overtime.

The guy's blood got on his hands, but Craig ignored it.

"Get on the floor and cover me," he said to his wife and rushed at the study door, the guy's body a shield ahead of him.

Just before he reached the door he tossed the body as hard as he could, using his running momentum to get the body to hit the door halfway up and at a good speed.

Then Craig dropped to the carpet, rifle pointed ahead.

The body smashed open the study door and was instantly peppered with bullets, making the dead man jerk and flip his arms as he dropped.

Craig had his gun up and firing before the body was out of the way.

Almost instantly the gunfire from inside the study stopped. A moment later there was the sound of a gun hitting the floor.

Craig dove over the dead man and rolled, coming up with his rifle facing Charles Robins' scared face and his shaking hand that was holding a small pistol.

To Robins' right was the guard who had been firing, now slumped in, and bleeding all over, an expensive leather chair.

"I would suggest you drop that gun now," Bonnie said, moving to cover her husband. "I would love to pull this trigger and blow those tiny brains of yours all over your desk."

Charles glanced at her, then dropped his gun like it was suddenly too hot to hold.

Craig used the barrel of his rifle to kick the gun onto the floor.

"Now," he said to Robins, "tell your men to drop their weapons and surrender."

Robins hesitated until Craig raised his rifle and pointed it at the man's head. Then Robins picked up a small communications unit and said, "Attention. This is Robins. Drop your weapons now. Cease fire."

Slowly the noise of gunfire died off, replaced by a wonderful silence filled only by distant sirens.

"Tell them to put their hands on their heads and walk toward the nearest cop until told otherwise," Craig said.

Robins hesitated.

"Oh, please let me shoot him," Bonnie said, moving up and putting her gun against the side of his head.

"Oh, I kind of like this side of you," Craig said, smiling at her.

"Let me pull the trigger and see how hot it gets me," she said, winking at him.

Robins instantly moved to do as Craig had ordered, repeating his words exactly. He clearly believed Bonnie would kill him.

"Now what?" Robins asked as he finished.

"Now we shoot you," Bonnie said, raising her gun again.

"She's just kidding," Craig said, smiling at the sick look on Robins' face. "But I won't hesitate. So come on out from behind there and sit at the feet of your dead man there."

Robins did as Craig told him until he stood over his dead guard. Then he turned and shook his head. "I can't do that."

"You caused his death," Craig said. "Seems you owe him a little company. Now sit down."

Craig jammed his rifle into Robins' chest and the man dropped to the floor.

Craig took the dead man's arms and placed them around Robins' neck, as if the man was giving his boss a hug from behind. Blood dripped down the front of Robins' shirt from the man's hand.

"Now isn't that sweet?" Bonnie asked Craig.

Craig couldn't think of a better thing to have happen to the man who wanted Senator Knight dead. And who had ordered his men to fire on police.

Charles Robins looked as if he might throw up at any minute, but with Bonnie's rifle leveled on his chest, he didn't move.

Ten minutes later Hagar and a dozen others swarmed into the room. Once they saw that Craig and Bonnie had it under control, they stopped and all but two of them moved off to finish checking the house.

"I was wondering why they suddenly stopped firing and gave up," Hagar said.

Craig pointed at where Robins still sat with the dead guard's arms around his neck. "He just needed a little convincing is all. And Bonnie is a real good convincer."

Craig smiled at his wife as she nodded her thanks.

"Does he know about Senator Knight's press conference yet?" Hagar asked.

"When is that scheduled?" Bonnie asked, smiling at the startled look from Robins.

"Eight eastern time," Hagar said. "Just about any moment now."

"Well," Craig said, "Bonnie turn it on while someone reads Mr. Robins his rights."

Hagar got down on one knee in front of Robins, and without moving the dead man's arms off the guy's shoulders, read Charles Robins his rights.

A moment later, on CNN, the serious face of Senator Knight appeared and began to talk.

For a short moment Charles Robins just stared at the screen, then slowly he closed his eyes.

"Ain't justice wonderful?" Craig asked, listening as Senator Knight thanked him and Bonnie for saving his life.

CHAPTER TWENTY-NINE

Monday, April 10th
6:36 a.m.

THE LIMO PULLED through the gate and out onto the tarmac of the Scottsdale airport, stopping beside the two private jets just as the sun was breaking over the hills to the east. A moment later the man Charles Robins called Bill finished his last phone call. He hung up the phone, then flipped closed the laptop computer he had been holding on his lap.

"Well?" Grant asked.

Bill looked across the private area of the limo at his old friend Grant and smiled.

"Done?" Grant asked.

"Done," Bill said. "We've just moved over sixty-seven million of Charles Robins' company's money to varied accounts, and then on to other numbered accounts. It will be moved automatically another hundred times, in varied amounts, before it finally settles in our accounts."

"As always no one can trace it?" Grant asked.

"Trust me," Bill said, "if someone does try to trace it, it will look like Charles did it himself. And the money will be gone. Hell, it will take a team of auditors years to find everything that's missing."

Grant laughed, the sound filling the limo. "The man was just too stupid for words."

"That he was. And I must say, it was a pleasure taking him for every penny."

"It almost makes taking orders from the idiot for four years worth it."

"Sixty-seven million?" Bill said, laughing. "I'd say that was worth it. You got us access to everything the man owned, every password, every account. And the guy let you." Bill shook his head at the craziness of it all.

Grant laughed, his big frame shaking. "Sure hope those two nice cops from Seattle got out of that firefight alive. She was a looker."

"I'm sure they did," Bill said. "They were smart enough to save the Senator, they're smart enough to get out of Robins' house, I'm sure."

"I sure wanted to tell old Robins about Senator Knight being just fine in Washington, D.C.," Grant said, laughing.

"If he doesn't know by now," Bill said, "he will shortly."

The two men laughed again and climbed out of the limo.

Bill looked at the two planes. One jet waited for him, the other for Grant. They were headed in two different directions.

In a matter of hours they would both be far out of the reach of Charles Robins and the FBI. In a matter of days they would both have new identities and enough money to last a very long time.

"Well, friend," Grant said, shaking his hand. "When will I see you again?"

"Oh, a year or so. As soon as I find another sucker like Robins. I'll be in touch."

"Take your time," Grant said. "I think I've got enough to last for a few years."

The man who had been called Bill laughed.

They let go of the handshake and turned for their jets.

It was the third time they had done this to a stupid, greedy businessman like Robins. They both knew it wouldn't be the last. They enjoyed the score too much. It made life worth living for both of them.

Bill's jet left the runway first, followed a minute later by Grant's.

In the air one jet turned west, the other south.

EPILOGUE

Friday, April 14th
10:12 p.m.

MONDAY HAD TURNED into a day from hell for both of them. Bonnie could not remember a day like it before. They had had no sleep and millions of questions to answer, forms to fill out, details to go over.

And all while trying to understand that Maxwell had been killed.

Bonnie found his death almost impossible to believe for some reason. The guy seemed like he always had everything under control. But clearly he had made one mistake, and that was walking into the line of fire of that estate's front gate.

Hagar had told them that he was lucky to get back when the firing started.

Bonnie still hadn't believed Maxwell was dead until the funeral on Thursday. Then finally she had allowed herself to cry for the man she had only known a short time.

By six in the evening on Monday they had been allowed to return to their hotel room for a shower and change of clothes.

But Hagar had had a car bring them right back to the station.

By midnight Monday they had finished almost everything that needed to be done immediately, and were allowed to go back to the hotel to sleep.

By eight the next morning they were back at the station.

The hearings and interviews seemed to stretch forever. Over and over again, both together and separately, Bonnie and Craig had answered questions about what had happened the entire weekend.

All day Tuesday, all day Wednesday, after Maxwell's funeral on Thursday, and then even more questions on Friday morning.

Finally, Friday afternoon they had been set free. Bonnie had felt numb and more tired than she had felt in years.

On Wednesday, Charles Robins had been arraigned on more counts than Bonnie believed was possible to charge one man with. And fifty-six of his men were under charges of attempted murder, murder, and so on. Besides Maxwell, ten others had died, all Robins' men. Ten cops and two FBI agents had been wounded, but only one seriously.

The firefight, combined with Senator Knight's sudden appearance in Washington, made all the national news and created a massive media stir around the police headquarters in Scottsdale that didn't die off until Thursday.

Somewhere in the middle of Monday afternoon, Bonnie remembered talking to her boss in Seattle, telling her they wouldn't be back for at least a week. Her boss completely understood.

Now it was Friday again. One week after they had first arrived for a weekend golf tournament. They had both taken naps in the afternoon and got out on the putting green and practiced for a few hours after dinner. But neither of their hearts were into playing golf.

As it was getting dark, Craig had suggested they go for a walk.

One week from the time they went for that first walk and overheard a conversation that changed a lot of lives.

"You sure you want to?" Bonnie asked, smiling at her husband. "You remember what happened last time we did that?"

"Sex?" he asked. "I remember sex on warm grass under bright stars."

She took his hand. "I think there's a rock out there with our name on it."

They strolled silently along the dark path.

She forced herself to not think about the events of the week. It was almost impossible to do, but somehow she wanted to get back to that feeling of just walking in the dark, enjoying Craig's company, and thinking about making love.

He held her hand and every so often would squeeze it.

But he said nothing either.

Seemingly, much faster than the first time they had made the walk in the dark, they reached the big rock.

Bonnie pulled him off the path and out onto the grass of the fairway.

She let go of his hand, kicked her shoes off, and laid down, enjoying the feeling of the warm grass against her skin.

They were both numb and she knew it, but somehow they had to come back to what they had together, put the week behind them and start new again.

She watched as he stood over her, his shape outlined against the stars.

"What are you thinking?" she asked, her voice sounding louder than she had expected in the night.

"Just how beautiful you are," he said.

"Really?" she asked, smiling up at him.

"Really," he said.

"And nothing else?" she asked.

"Just that you have too many clothes on for such a warm night."

She laughed, raised her hips and slid her shorts down and off her legs.

"How's that?"

"Better," he said, still just standing over her.

She sat up slightly and pulled her top over her head.

"Better," he said again.

She unhooked her bra and took it off.

"Getting close," he said.

She slid her panties off her legs and tossed them away.

"Perfect," he said.

She stood and gave him a long, hard kiss, then pushed him down onto the ground. "Now who has too many clothes on?"

They went through the same routine until he was nude and lying under her spread feet.

"I love this view," he said, staring up at her.

"Things don't look so bad from here," she said.

They stayed like that for a moment, then slowly she eased down on top of him, letting him hold her, letting him make love to her.

Finally, things were again right in the world.

They were together and that was all that mattered.

~

Now Available
from all your favorite booksellers
in trade paper and electronic editions.

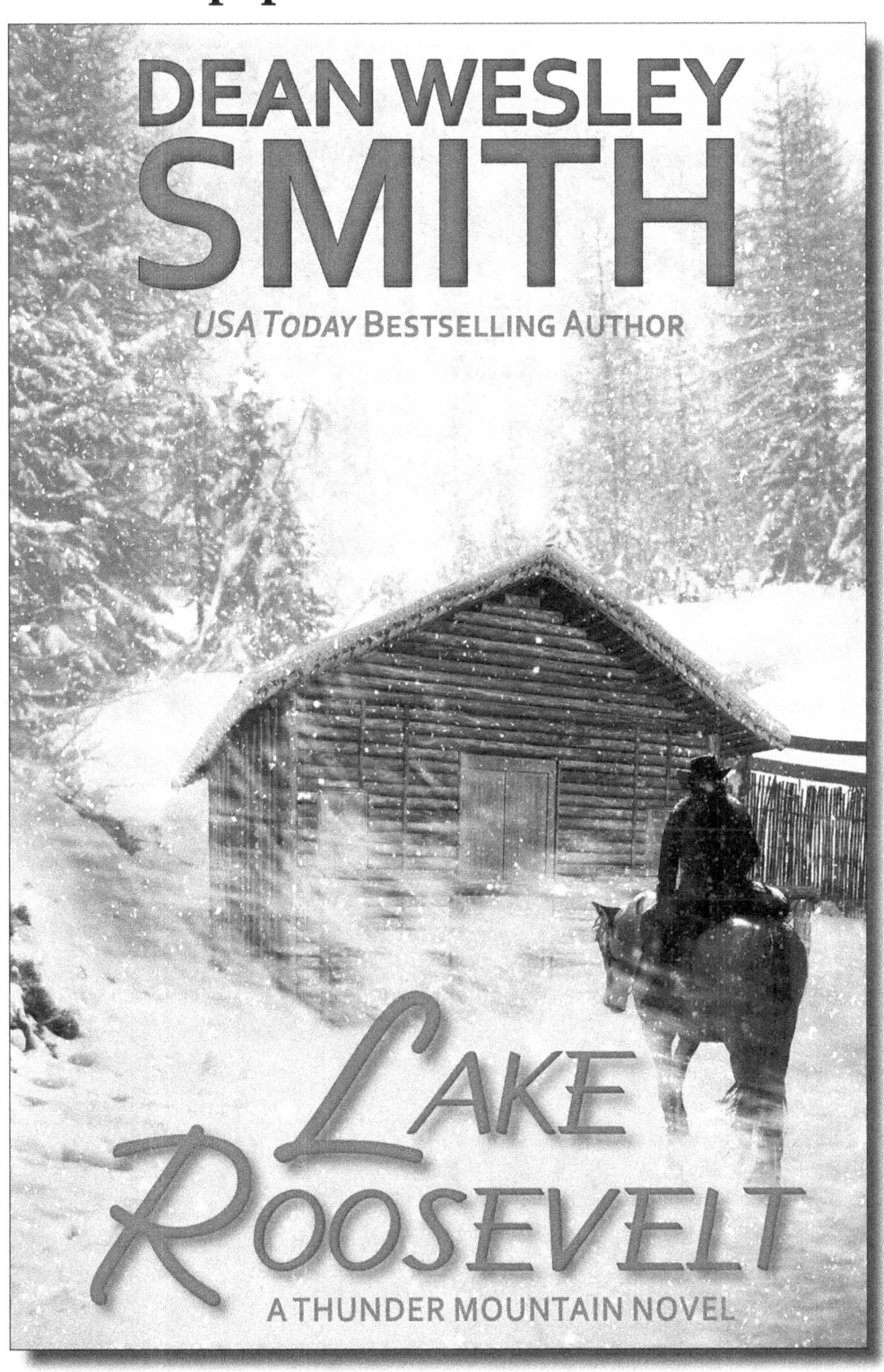

DEAN WESLEY
SMITH

USA Today BESTSELLING AUTHOR

LAKE
ROOSEVELT

A THUNDER MOUNTAIN NOVEL

Dean Wesley Smith

USA *Today* Bestselling Writer

CT#2

A perfect wife.
A perfect home.
A not-so-perfect husband.
What possibly
could go wrong?

Call Me Unfixable

A Bryant Street Story

A perfect wife. A perfect home. A not-so-perfect husband.

What possibly could go wrong?

As a trial lawyer, Craig could face any situation and make it work. But facing his controlling wife and her lover (while they drank wine in his bed) turned out to need more than just a good plan.

Craig needed to believe in his actions, every action, no matter how small.

Or large.

CALL ME UNFIXABLE
A Bryant Street Story

ACT ONE

I SAT in my brand-new green Lexus on the hot pavement of Bryant Street and stared at the front door of my home across the lush and expensive green lawn, always perfectly kept, of course.

The car's engine idled almost silently and the air conditioning blew cold.

Before any rough day in court, as a major trial lawyer, I always sat in my car and made sure I was completely in character. The worst thing I could do in a courtroom was to have sudden doubts, or fall out of my belief system.

I thought of it as going on stage. I had to be completely in my character, completely submerged in the part I needed to play.

And that's what I had to do now. I had to stay in the part, in character. I couldn't let a stray thought break my concentration.

I again stared at the house. Right now the state-of-the-art sprinkler system was giving the lawn "just a taste" to keep it fresh looking even in the August heat. Most of the watering was done at night.

That stupid piece of green lawn had been taken out and replaced four times because Salina, my wife, wanted it to look better. Four different times it had been carefully rolled into place, carefully cut, carefully everything. And "carefully" meant expensive.

The brick planters along the front of the house always had to be perfect as well, present the perfect picture to the world of a happy, perfect home in our little subdivision. The perfect flowers had to be planted carefully in each planter for each of Portland, Oregon's seasons. Those flowers got replaced every two months, even if some of the old ones were still blooming.

And even worse, I had spent more money than I could ever imagine on slug poison because Salina had read an article about how slugs were bad in this part of the country.

Our lawn and planters, plus parts of the garage and the basement, were pure death to any poor slug that happened to wander into the yard. And who knew what all that poison was doing to other animals unlucky enough to venture across the line into Salina's perfect point-four acres in the suburbs.

Salina had loved her home, her yard, her plants, her furniture, her clothes, her dishes, her kitchen, everything she touched. She had tried to make everything perfect.

Even me.

But I was the one thing she could never make perfect, or convince to spend enough of my own money on myself to become what she considered perfect.

I was the one flaw in her perfectly ordered and maintained life.

She could spend my money on everything else, but I had drawn the line with changing myself.

And that had become our biggest problem. I just didn't care enough to be perfect. I kind of liked myself the way I was. I stood six-two, worked out so I had no excess weight at thirty-three, unlike most of my friends and co-workers in the law firm. And I had a smile that many said lit up a room.

But Salina said my nose was crooked and it needed to be fixed. It was crooked, slightly, because of a skiing accident up on Mount Hood when I was twenty-four, a year after I married Salina. But I liked it. I thought it gave my face character.

Salina saw it as an imperfection.

And she was big into yoga, but no chance in hell I was going to do that. I ran in the gym down near the office and played golf in the summer and skied in the winter. No way I was going to sit and try to get my damned leg over my head.

Salina was into fine wines and had me spend a fortune for a wine cellar dug under the house. That cellar had been one of our biggest fights. Of course, she won.

The wine cellar was tighter than most bank vaults and controlled with its own environmental system. Expensive didn't begin to describe that room.

I hated most wines. I liked a good micro-brew and had a fridge in the perfectly clean garage that kept my beer.

And she had wanted me to learn to like the cultural stuff around Portland, but all I had wanted to attend was a University of Oregon Ducks football game.

So after years of marriage, I had become an abomination to Salina. She wouldn't allow me to touch her and she seldom talked to me unless she wanted something from me or wanted to criticize something I was doing, eating, or watching.

So today, as planned, I would end it.

If the plan worked as set out, Salina's little perfect world would come crashing down around her head.

I was in perfect form, ready to go on stage and play my part. It felt good to do this preparation time again.

I glanced up the street at the deep-blue convertible Cadillac parked like it belonged to the house three doors away. But Jimmy, my private detective and best friend, told me it belonged to Percy Samuels.

Salina and Percy.

Such a perfect-sounding couple.

Percy owned what seemed like a swank health spa in the Pearl District downtown, but Jimmy told me he was completely broke. Percy lived in a sloppy apartment littered with Coors beer cans and was within one month of having that fancy blue car repossessed.

On top of that, the IRS had liens on his business and were about to strike, a source told me.

That source, of course, was Jimmy.

Everything I knew about Salina and Percy came though Jimmy.

Jimmy and I had been friends since college and he knew how to dig out information in both legal and illegal ways. We skied together in the winter and played golf together every Saturday.

And now, with everything, we spent almost all our time together.

He only stood five-four, but was the most powerful small man I had ever met. I might be ten inches taller and weigh more, but not a chance in the world would I ever want to take him on in a fight.

Jimmy often found me information for a client I couldn't legally use, but that illegal information usually pointed to something I could use.

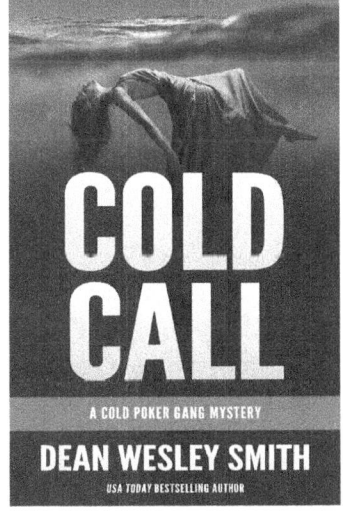

First Three Cold Poker Gang Novels
Available at your favorite booksellers.

Way back when I asked him to look into what Salina was doing, all he did was laugh. Then he said, "I was wondering when the sex was going to turn bad and you were going to grow a pair in dealing with her."

So Jimmy did his best and found all sorts of information that would allow me to kick Salina down the road and not pay her a cent.

Salina and Percy had been lovers now for six months. Usually in the afternoons when they knew I was going to be in court.

I had to admit, that was smart.

Of course, that backfired on them, all their careful planning.

And Salina had been stashing some cash away, which I had managed to make vanish out of her accounts.

Jimmy managed to get all our joint accounts locked down tight and all her credit cards cancelled.

Salina was as broke as her lover Percy.

I looked out over the perfect green lawn saturated in snail bait. It was time for me to play this game, walk on this stage, and go into that house once again. I already had a wonderful condominium downtown, only blocks from my office. And I liked it, had furnished it the way I wanted a place furnished, including the biggest screen one of the rooms could handle.

Percy and Salina were in their perfect world. They just didn't know it.

I almost felt sorry for him. Her, I never would have a moment's regret.

My cell phone in my pocket was on and open, connected to my best friend. "You there, Jimmy?"

"Waiting just around the corner as usual, Craig," Jimmy's deep voice came back strong. "Just leave the line open and

I'll make sure I get everything. I'll come running if there is an ounce of trouble."

"Thanks, buddy," I said.

Jimmy played his part in our little play perfectly. You couldn't ask for a better friend.

Leaving the connection open in my pocket so that Jimmy could hear, I moved from the car and out into the sun.

For Portland, the day was warm, promising to top out in the mid-nineties.

Taking a deep breath to steady my nerves, just as I did when going into court, I moved up my front walk, my leather dress shoes making faint clicking sounds on the concrete that sounded like it echoed up and down the street.

I wasn't actually sure they made any sound, but I sure hoped they did, at least a little. In this play, I wanted them to make the noise.

Then, moving as silently as I could, I went through the front door and stood just inside. It felt like I was sweating slightly in the sudden coolness of the air. I wasn't sure if I actually was or if I just wanted to believe I was.

I had done it. I was inside.

I stayed very still to try to discover what I could hear.

Of course, there was nothing. I had done so much build-up to this, like planning a major court case, my nerves were almost out of control.

It made me feel alive, which I loved.

"You okay, Craig?" Jimmy's voice came faintly from my phone in my pocket.

I whispered. "Inside the house. Give me a minute."

The play continued.

I started down the hallway toward our master bedroom, working hard to make as little noise as possible.

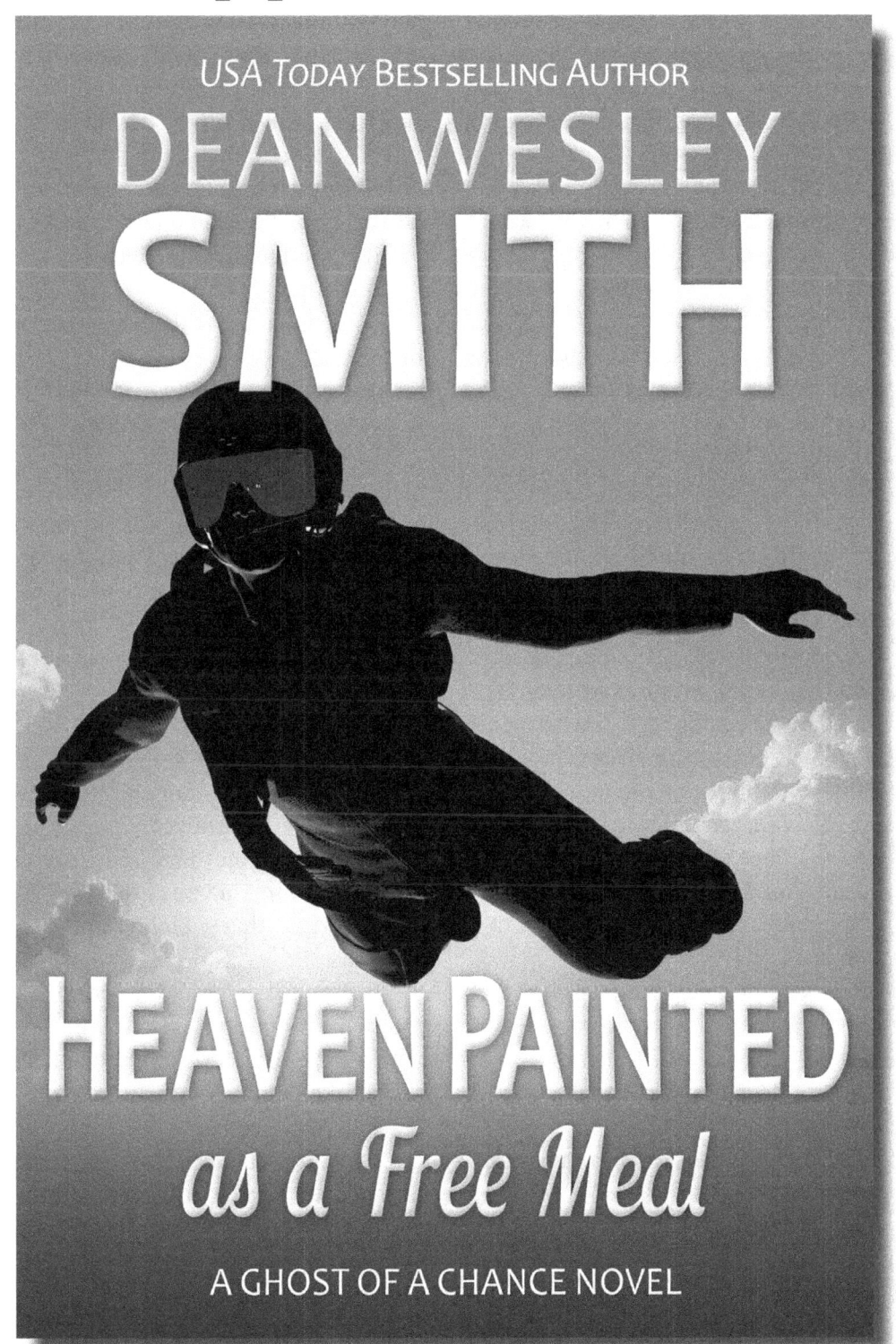

No one there.

The huge room was in perfect condition, the bed made, the blinds open, the summer light filling the pink and orange space that was Salina's idea of a perfect master bedroom.

I felt dizzy, so I made myself take a couple deep breaths until the swirling passed. I couldn't let the images of anything but today come into my mind. I had to stay firmly in character or this would not work yet again.

After a moment, I went back to the game of searching for my wife and her lover, making sure I stayed right on the script Jimmy and I had worked out.

That was critical.

Of course I found nothing.

The house was empty.

I carefully opened a cabinet and took one of my old coffee mugs out and placed it on the counter, just where it wasn't supposed to be.

I stared at it for a moment, almost stunned, but again working to keep myself in character, acting as if what I had just done was perfectly normal.

Salina would have never allowed that to happen. It was something out of place, something not perfect, so if I left the mug there, she would have cleaned it up.

And then I would have heard about it for an hour.

"A place for everything and everything in its place," she would repeat over and over.

I tended to agree with that now for her.

I stared at the mug for a moment longer, savoring the victory.

Then I walked through the house again, looking in all four bedrooms, in my study, in her private room. Then I went down the narrow flight of stairs and into the wine cellar, making sure that I covered everything.

I had come to love the wine cellar and actually stood for a short time with one hand on the wine racks and just smiled at all the wine I had bought Salina that now she would never drink.

Then, as if I did the action every day, I took some slug bait from a trap in a back corner and spread it into the small wall heater. Then I turned on the wall heater.

It started to crackle. Perfect.

It worked.

I had managed to do at least that much this year.

I caught myself and made myself stay in perfect character for the play.

I continued my search.

No one.

The house had a feel of emptiness to it, and now that I was looking around again, I could see faint signs of dust in certain places.

The cleaning services were clearly not doing a good job.

I moved into the kitchen area and looked out over the living room. A very empty place, even though it was full of very expensive furniture.

I talked in the direction of my shirt pocket. "Jimmy, no one home."

"Be right there, buddy," he said and hung up.

I stood there on the edge of the living room staring around at the empty house with all the perfect furniture that had never felt like a home to me.

The play needed to continue.

Every detail needed to be perfect if this was to work. So I headed down the hall to make the motion of checking for her car. I had to stay on stage. That's what kept me grounded.

It was the only thing that mattered.

As I expected, her car was still parked there.

I went back to the dark granite kitchen counter as Jimmy came through the front door and moved over beside me.

He had a very worried look on his face.

I gave him a thumbs up and pointed to the mug.

"So where are they?" I asked him, indicating the empty room, continuing the script we had set up.

"Damn," Jimmy said. "I was so hoping that this year you would remember."

"Remember what?" I asked.

Jimmy started into his part of the script.

"Three years ago Salina and Percy figured out that you were going to kick her down the road. So they tried to poison you with slug bait."

I shook my head. I needed to pretend I had no memory of any of that. "What happened?"

"You managed to fight them off and get outside and call me and I managed to get you to a hospital. You were in a coma for almost four months."

I said nothing since I had no lines in this play and Jimmy went on talking, telling me a fantastic story that I knew wasn't possible.

Yet part of me wanted to believe it was possible, because it was such a nice story. A lot better than the truth I wanted to believe.

And a ton better than the real truth.

"When Salina and Percy realized you were going to live and they were going to be arrested, they made a run for Mexico. They didn't make it. She's still in jail in California for some crime they did down there and will be for another ten years before coming back up here to face charges for trying to kill you."

Jimmy could really tell a wild story and he had this one very well practiced after the years of telling it to me.

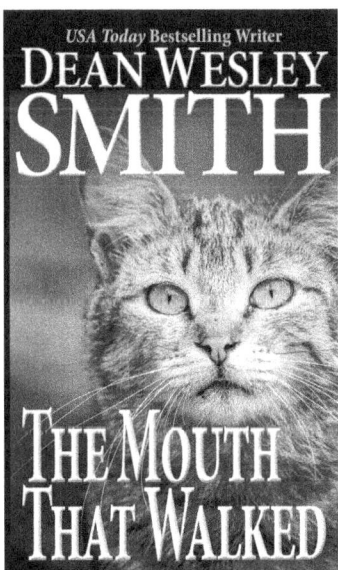

Some Classic Dean Wesley Smith Stories
Available at your favorite booksellers.

Again I said nothing, staying in the part of a person who couldn't remember anything that happened.

"When you woke up," Jimmy said, "you had only half your stomach left and no memory of anything. You were convinced instead that you and Salina were divorced and that she's completely gone. You just won't seem to believe anything else."

I would have never thought it would have been possible for Salina to try to kill me. I would have never thought the perfect woman in the perfect house with the perfect life had that sort of thing in her. Yet, in the real world, she got rid of everything that wasn't perfect or fixed it, so getting rid of me would have seemed logical to her.

It sure made for a great story for Jimmy to feed me to keep me on stage and solidly in this play.

Jimmy just went on telling me the story that he told me every year at this point. "You've kept this house perfect, just as Salina would have wanted it, even though you never come here except today. Every year, on this day, you come back here to tell her you are kicking her out. And I come with you to help."

I honestly loved this play. It was so real.

And Jimmy made his part of the story very convincing.

"And it happens like this every year?" I asked.

"Every damn year," Jimmy said, answering my question.

He was standing beside me, looking very worried.

"I think I'm going to be all right. The memories of the last few years seem to be coming back."

"Seriously?" Jimmy asked, his square face set in frown lines.

"Yup, I think I remember now," I said. "At least most of it. Still some foggy places."

Jimmy's large brown eyes just looked even more worried.

"So what do you remember?" Jimmy asked. "Everything. Run me through it."

And so the second act of our little play started.

ACT TWO

"I DON'T remember Salina serving me the slug bait," I said.

Again, this was just like being in a courtroom defending a client. My beliefs needed to be distant from my actions. I could never allow any belief but the belief I needed that day in court to come to the surface.

And that's the way I was playing this.

"I do remember a doctor telling me that the kind of coma I had gone into can cause some brain damage, especially to memory."

Jimmy nodded, staying on his part of the script and I could feel all this becoming solid and very real.

I smiled at my friend. "I remember you and I were planning on coming here later in the week to catch Salina and Percy doing the bed-sheet mambo and kick them out. But it never happened. Right?"

Jimmy nodded and said nothing.

I looked around the perfectly decorated big house.

And just like I was supposed to do in this part of the story, I did not mention to my best friend that Salina and Percy were behind the shelves in the wine cellar. That was the script. So I went along with the game he and I were playing to bring me back to the world.

We had tried this same game for the last couple years. Same game every year. Same script. We were getting better at it.

This very well might be the year.

"I have no memory of Salina being in jail however. Didn't she and Percy just vanish?"

"They did." Jimmy shrugged. "I've thought that they were better off gone from the start."

"But I do like the story of her being in jail," I said and Jimmy smiled.

If I really had memory issues.

As I did every year at this point in our little play, I asked the question once more. "Any idea where they are?"

Jimmy shook his head.

I looked around. "So why do I keep this place?"

Jimmy shrugged and said his lines perfectly. "Maybe it's because you think Salina and Percy might return if you keep it."

"That's just flat silly," I said, smiling at my friend and getting a smile in return.

I knew for a fact that they had never left.

"So you are making progress," Jimmy said.

"Real progress," I said.

I picked up the mug and put it back in the cabinet.

A place for everything and everything in its place.

Jimmy just nodded and smiled.

Salina and Percy were drinking wine naked the day I walked in on them, four days before I drank the slug poison to cover for me killing them, making people believe they had tried to kill me instead. She loved her wine cellar so much. She and her lover are now happy together down there.

A place for everything and everything in its place.

The wine cellar is a little smaller than it was originally designed, but I doubt anyone will notice.

"That's a hell of a story you tell me every year," I said to Jimmy, pretending I now remembered how much of a story it really was.

"I'll do anything to help," he said.

"Oh, you do help," I said.

And thus started the third act of our little play as we walked out into the afternoon sunshine.

ACT THREE

SALINA AND PERCY were sitting there, in my car, Percy behind the steering wheel.

Right on schedule, as they always were. Salina did not believe in being late for anything.

I was now in perfect courtroom mode. I was deep in the belief of the case, knew what I had to believe and had tossed out all other beliefs. The ability to do that, stay completely submerged into the play in the courtroom, was why I had won so many cases.

After a moment Salina and Percy got out and started up the walk toward the front door, neither saying a word to the other.

Clearly the sex was going bad between them and poor old Percy was starting to understand what kind of woman he had gotten hooked up with.

Jimmy and I stepped to one side and let them pass, then followed them back into the house.

We had done the same thing every year, but this year I hoped things would be different.

I made myself stop and not think that way. I needed to stay solidly on the script.

"So how come we just don't sell this place?" Percy asked. "We could sure use the money."

I was stunned. They had gone through most of my money and insurance in just three years. That was a lot of money.

I pushed that thought down as well and got back into my belief system.

Salina turned to him and gave him that nasty look she used to give me. "And have someone discover the bodies in the wine cellar?"

"That would be nice," I said.

Jimmy laughed.

Of course Salina and Percy didn't hear me. They just headed for the wine cellar.

Percy pulled the door open and said, "Wow, that's a smell."

Jimmy glanced at me and smiled. He knew at that moment that I had managed to get the slug bait on the heater and turn it on.

"It's in your head," Salina said, pushing past him and going down the stairs. "The bodies can't smell, you fool. We wrapped them up too tightly in layers of plastic and they are behind a very solid wall, remember?"

"How could I ever forget," Percy said, following her.

They went down the narrow stairs to check on where they had buried me and Jimmy behind the wine racks after killing us three years ago today.

I turned to my best friend. "I seemed to have left the door to the wine cellar open in my check of the house."

"Better close it," he said. "You know there are expensive bottles of wine down there you wouldn't want stolen."

So as if I was still playing the game of looking for Salina and her lover, I moved to the wine cellar door, pushed it closed, and locked it.

Everything in its place.

Then I turned off the lights and went to the breaker box and flipped the breaker switch, leaving the breaker for the heater down there on.

Jimmy just cheered beside me.

"Holy crap, we did it!" he shouted, jumping up and down in his excitement.

Actually, I was pretty stunned as well.

I could feel myself smiling and smiling.

The two people who had killed Jimmy and me were now locked with our bodies in the wine cellar in the dark.

And they were breathing very poison air.

A moment later I could hear Percy banging on the door shouting to be let out. His voice did not sound like he was much in control.

Behind him I heard Salina coughing. Then she said, "Idiot! Why did you pull the door closed behind you?"

"I didn't," Percy said, his voice a couple octaves higher than normal.

Salina coughed a few more times, then said, "Break it down, you fool."

The door pounded hard, but I remembered that when we had that wine cellar built, Salina wanted the best material and the best locks since we were going to have a lot of expensive wine down there.

She had said that many, many times to me during construction and in the arguments leading up to construction.

So the door held and then after a moment there was a loud crashing sound as two bodies tumbled back down the stairs.

And then it was silent.

"I'll be," Jimmy said, laughing. "We did it! We actually did it!"

I could feel this immense sense of satisfaction. Three years of practicing the scripts to make sure I felt connected to the real world. Three years of returning here to this house I hated on the day she had killed me and my best friend. We had caught her making love to Percy, but we didn't expect the gun she had bought and had in the drawer beside her.

And I didn't know about her trips to the gun range to learn how to use the thing.

Three years waiting for revenge.

And now it was here.

Outside I could hear the faint sounds of a siren headed this way.

"She got off a 911 call," Jimmy said, suddenly looking worried again.

"They won't be alive by the time the police find them," I said, smiling at my best friend.

"I hope you are right," he said.

"I am," I said. "Head back to your waiting spot for a minute, would you? We need to start the play over just one more time. I want to make sure they find our bodies as well."

He looked puzzled, but just nodded and then vanished.

A moment later his voice came over my phone inside my suit coat. "I'm here if you need me."

I said in the general direction of my pocket, "Listen and enjoy."

I put myself back in the courtroom, back in the belief that I was alive and could actually move physical objects without thinking about it.

I believed it more than I had ever believed in a case.

I was here to look for Salina and Percy in bed together.

I looked around the home I hated, then moved over to the front door and opened it and left it standing open for Jimmy to come in. Just in case I had trouble when I found Salina and Percy in bed together.

Some Classic Dean Wesley Smith Stories
Available at your favorite booksellers.

Staying solidly in my belief of where and when I was, I went back through the house, looking for Salina and her boyfriend. Making sure that with every thought, every belief, I would find them alive and making love.

Of course, I didn't find them.

As I finished my search of the back bedrooms, I heard a call from the front door. "Police! Anyone here?"

I had heard no sounds at all from the wine cellar in almost five minutes. So on the way toward the front I clicked back on the breaker lights for the wine cellar.

Then focusing as hard as I could to stay in the act of our little play and not get caught for murdering my wife and her lover and putting their bodies behind the wine racks, I went forward to greet the police.

I had to play this one perfectly. Just like a summary statement in front of a jury.

I had done it a thousand times. Once more, with flourish this time.

"Hello," I said and two young cops both turned to me.

Wow, they were making patrol officers young these days. Both looked like they were right out of college, if that. One even had a face of pimples.

I pointed at the door just off the kitchen. "My wife and her boyfriend are dead down there in the wine cellar."

They both just looked at me, clearly stunned and trying to process what I had just said. Then the one with the bad skin said, "Did you do it?"

What a stupid question for a policeman to ask, but I was glad he did. He played right into my plan perfectly.

"Of course I did," I said. "I killed them. But there are two bodies behind one of the wine racks that she killed. Make sure you take care of those as well."

Then, while they stood there stunned, I walked for the last time out the front door of the house Salina built and I had come to hate.

"Hey, wait a minute!" one cop said behind me and turned to follow.

But I was gone.

"Where did he go?" the one cop asked.

Quickly they went in different directions around the house, looking for me while calling in for backup.

But they would never find me, at least this part of me. I hoped they found my body down there behind the wine rack.

But this part of me was back in my reality. I was off stage, out of the belief that I had needed to touch the few things I had needed to touch. I knew and believed now that I was only a ghost.

And beside me, Jimmy was laughing.

"Well played," he said. "Who knew you could act like that."

"I'm a trial lawyer, remember," I said. "I can believe anything if I really need to."

"Oh, yeah," he said. "Who would have thought as a ghost I would need a lawyer."

Laughing, we turned and walked down Bryant Street.

I had no idea where we were going, but anywhere was better than staying in that home with that woman.

Now Available
from all your favorite booksellers
in trade paper and electronic editions.

USA TODAY BESTSELLING AUTHOR

DEAN WESLEY SMITH

A DOC HILL THRILLER

DEAD MONEY

""[An] exhilarating political poker thriller."
—*Midwest Book Reviews*

Dean Wesley Smith

USA Today **Bestselling Writer**

Sometimes dreams
share a dark side
with death.

Clicking
Sticks

When the girl next door... the girl haunting your dreams for years... comes to you for help, you know things may change.

Just maybe you might get a dream to come true.

But sometimes dreams share a dark side with death.

CLICKING STICKS

ONE

ANNIE.
Five simple letters that strike fear into me like I am an American Flag and Betsy Ross is a serial killer coming at me with scissors. Annie. That simple, traditional name brings images to my mind of slightly too large breasts, narrow hips, and a smile as cold as a hooker's zipper.

Annie, the cheerleader, the president of my senior class, the smart girl who is destined to become "something" or "someone" if she can keep those tight little red cheerleader panties up long enough to not let her loser boyfriend get her pregnant.

Annie, the girl I've been in love with since the first grade when she and her parents moved in next door. The actual girl next door, the same one that used to join our baseball games and who helped us build a brick fort in the masonry plant lot one summer.

Annie, the first girl I ever kissed because her sister told her she had to when we both stood under mistletoe. For the first three, maybe four years that she lived next door, she was just Annie. A good friend, someone fun to be with.

Then she changed.

She became a "girl."

Now Annie scared the fuck out of me every time she smiled when we met in the hall, every time she said, "Hi, Brad," in that bet-you-want-to-see-my-tits voice.

Sure, I wanted to see them. No straight boy in the school didn't. I'd wanted to see them since they started becoming an issue in the 4th grade, when she started to wear that first bra a year before most other girls had to. That first year I had even asked her to see them, and she might have let me if her damn sister hadn't been home early that day.

Annie lived next door to me and her bedroom window faced mine over what seemed like six miles of grass and a chain-link fence. A couple of times I had caught glimpses of her in her underwear and bra through her bedroom window when the summer night was hot and she had left her blinds open. And I want to say right now that there is no truth to the rumor I used to spend nights camped under that window. I only went over that fence once. Maybe twice.

Too damn scary. And I never saw anything but bra.

I suppose I sound like a pansy-ass wimp-boy, talking about being so afraid of a simple cheerleader. Usually, I don't show fear. I ride motocross and can catch some pretty good air at times. And I've had other girlfriends, even gone out with Annie's best friend a few times. Girls don't worry me that much, and neither does getting hurt or even getting killed. Actually, not much in the world really scares me.

Except Annie.

And I might have gone all the way through the last year of high school and kept being afraid of her if not for her stupid-ass jock boyfriend. Rees.

Rees Trager, cliché. I figured he should have a shirt with that on it. Star of the football team, point guard for the Oregon State high school basketball champions, rich parents, not many brains, and not a single social skill to be found. Add that mixture in to an ego the size of his Hummer and a love of too much vodka and I figured Annie was doomed unless she ran like hell. But I sure wasn't going to be the one to mention that fact to her. I figured she was smart and would eventually see the light, or should I say, lack of light in old Rees's eyes.

I just didn't expect her to come running to me, dear old neighbor Brad, when she saw that light. But that was exactly what happened.

TWO

TWO IN THE MORNING, Thursday night, Friday morning.

I'd finishing cramming for a physics test and had just nodded off when someone knocked. Actually, tapped. Lightly. On my window.

I was dreaming of having Chinese dinner, and the skinny girl I was with was tapping her chopsticks on the table.

Tap. Tap. Tap. Tap.

Stop.

In my dream, her breasts grew and *they* knew how to use chopsticks to click on the table.

Tap. Tap. Tap. Tap.

Then a faint voice came from the window before the next tap.

"Brad?"

Even half asleep, even tired from cramming too damn many stupid equations into my head, I knew Annie's voice.

My dream of the breasts holding chop-sticks vanished like a good meal.

I scrambled out of bed like someone had just told me there were spiders under the sheets and got to the window without tripping or making enough noise to wake my parents. I cranked up the blinds be-fore I even gave a thought to what I was wearing, which was a motocross tee-shirt and blue-striped boxers.

Annie was standing in the grass, her head about level with my crotch through the glass window.

Okay, to be frank, I had dreamed of us being in this position with Annie more times than I could count. Just not like this. And yes, they were *that* kind of dreams, so sue me.

Annie stood there, arms crossed over her chest as if she were trying to hold those large breasts from making a break for it through the cold March night. Her long brown hair was really messed up, and from the faint light coming from the hallway behind me, I could tell that she'd been crying. She didn't have a coat on and she had to be freezing standing there in jeans and a thin blouse.

I slid the window open, bent down so my face was closer to hers through the screen and said the first thing that came to mind. "You all right?"

"No."

The no sounded weak and sort of shuddery, if that was a word. I couldn't believe that the woman I feared more than anything in the world was turning to me as a friend. Granted, I had tried to keep the outward appearance of how I felt for her friendly, but I just never figured I would be someone she would come to.

Yet here she stood. She must really be desperate and in trouble.

"Meet me in my driveway," I said. "I'll be right there."

She nodded and started around the back of the house.

I pulled the blind closed, then in a matter of less than a second, managed to pull on my jeans, grab my coat from the back of my chair, and then get a second coat for her from my closet. I think I got down the hallway without waking my parents, grabbed my mom's car keys as I went through the kitchen, and out through the side door.

My mom always left her car parked in the driveway, mostly because she said I kept too much of my bike "junk" in the garage and there wasn't room. I figured Annie and I could sit in her car and I could run it and keep us both warm.

I was about to sit in a parked car with the woman who scared me the most, who I had been in love with since the very first moment I noticed girls were different than boys.

It was a dream come true, again just not in the way I had hoped.

THREE

I HANDED Annie my second coat as I came around the side of the house and found her standing near my mother's red Buick.

"Thanks," she said, then needed my help to get it on. In the faint light from the street I could see that she had brown spots on her blouse, clearly blood. Something really ugly had happened to her.

"Jump in," I said, unlocking my mom's car with her automatic keys and then sliding in on the driver's side. I had only driven my dad's Chrysler on special dates, but my mom let me use her car all the time, so it felt like I was home behind the wheel.

Annie opened the passenger door and sort of climbed in, moving carefully as if she was afraid she might hurt herself. Under the bright dome lights I could see she was a mess. She had a couple of long scrapes along the side of her neck and from what I could tell she might end up with a pretty good black eye.

I didn't need to even ask. I knew at once that Mr. Jock, Mr. Big Man, Mr. Drunk, had finally shown his true colors to Annie.

But I had to be sure, so as she closed the door and stared at the dashboard in front of her, shaking, I asked, "Rees?"

She nodded slowly as the overhead light dimmed and went off.

I stuck the keys in the ignition and turned on the car. "It will warm up in a second."

"Thanks."

"Do you think you need a hospital?"

"No," she said, a little too quickly.

Then she turned to face me, tears running down her face in the faint light from the dashboard. "I need your help."

"Tell me what happened and I'll see what I can do." I surprised myself that my voice and my attitude seemed so in control when my stomach was doing a dance.

She stared at me for just about the rest of my life, thinking about my offer. I could feel my heart beating half out of my chest and I forced myself to keep breathing as regular as possible, just like I did at the start of any race. Even beat up and a mess, even in faint light, even with tears, she was still the most beautiful person I had ever known.

And this seemed like the first time she had ever really looked at me.

Finally, she nodded and started into her story. As anything with Rees, what had happened could have been planned by a bad writer on a cancelled sitcom. Out drinking with friends, he wanted her to go parking with him in his Hummer. She had said yes, and the two of them had ended up on the dirt maintenance road that ran beside the old New Trunk Canal.

Rees kept drinking and when she said no to his lewd advances, as she always did she claimed, he got angry.

"He pinned me against the door," she said, now really crying.

I wanted to reach out and hold her, but I stayed facing her, afraid to move.

"I kicked him between his legs and that stopped him," she said.

"I bet," I said, and managed to not make a rude comment about how she managed to hit such a small target.

"I got out and he came after me and started hitting me, holding me in the dirt and punching me."

Now she was really crying, her face in her hands. It was no wonder she had blood on her blouse.

Right about that moment, I almost put the car in reverse to take her to the hospital emergency room, but something about her story stopped me. It clearly wasn't over yet. It was missing the one element any good story needed. An ending.

"How did you get away?"

She didn't say anything.

"It's all right," I said after a few long minutes of her sobbing into her hands. "You can tell me."

She managed, between gasps for air, to say, "I grabbed a rock and I hit him in the side of the head."

Okay, now I had finally found some-thing that scared me more than Annie and her big tits. The image of Rees with a caved in skull.

Two in the morning, from the clock on my mom's dashboard.

Dark and silent in the neighborhood around us.

Annie, the girl of my dreams, sitting in the car beside me, sobbing, because she had just stopped her boyfriend from beating her up by hitting him with a rock.

And I was too damn afraid to ask the next question.

The heat had finally filled the car, maybe a little too much. I shut off the car but kept the key turned to keep the dash-board lights on.

Annie kept sobbing. I wanted to hold her.

I didn't want to hold her.

I was afraid to hold her, afraid to get really dragged into the mess that her night had become. There was no good outcome in my holding her. If Rees was still alive and caught me doing that, I would be dead. And if she had killed Rees, holding her might get me to do something real-ly stupid, like helping her cover up her crime. I had seen more than enough CSI shows to know that wasn't possible in this modern day and age.

Finally, I got up the nerve to ask.

"So what happened next? Where's Rees?"

"In the canal," she said, sobbing. Then she looked up at me and kept going. "I panicked and ran when he rolled off of me and down the bank into the canal. I killed him."

"How can you be sure?"

"I know. He didn't come up out of the water, only floated face down away from me."

With that she sobbed again, shudder-ing, her breasts bouncing like no breasts should bounce.

"That's why I need your help," she said. "I walked home. I figure I need to go back and make it look like an accident, like he had been drinking and ran off the road and hit his head and died."

"And you escaped with just bumps and bruises to explain him beating on you. Right?"

She nodded.

"Will you help me?"

She looked at me with those cheer-leader eyes.

Up until the moment she did the tap tap tap routine in my chopstick dream, I figured the only thing I was really afraid of was her. Now I knew there were many other things much worse. And hiding a crime from the cops was one.

No large breasts, no puppy-like love, was enough to make me do that. So I said what any normal, healthy, love-struck teenage boy would say when facing the woman of his wet dreams.

"Sure."

FOUR

SHE REACHED OUT and touched my arm and it was like an electrical charge had gone from her touch through my heart to my crotch. Mostly, just to my crotch.

I started my mom's car and backed out of the driveway, buckling up as I went. "What part of the canal bank road were you on?"

"Off of 23rd Street," she said, taking a deep breath and getting some of the old

Annie take-no-prisoner's attitude I knew so well.

"You know you should just report this, don't you? It was self-defense. No one would do anything to you."

"Except I'd always be known as the girl who killed her boyfriend. If we do this, I'm just the girl who lost her boyfriend in a tragic accident."

Not that I should have been surprised, but I was. She had done a lot of thinking in that long walk home. Cold, harsh thinking. And clearly she couldn't call any of her "true" friends to help her, so why not get that motorcycle kid from next door to do it.

I knew right then and there where I stood. And if I helped her, I'd have a lot of leverage in her life.

"You know," I said, as I headed down toward the canal, making sure my speed was right at the speed limit every moment, "I used to really have a crush on you."

"I know," she said.

My heart skipped a beat. She knew. I wasn't sure if that was good or bad.

"I always had this dream," I said, "of you letting me see you naked."

Okay, she kills someone and I suddenly have a ton of courage to tell her things I never would have said two hours ago. Go figure.

She actually laughed. She had just killed a guy and she laughed. Wow, she was either very cold or I was one hell of a comedian.

"You help me and you might get that wish."

"How about a little down payment?" I said, glancing around to make sure no cops were following. I really, really needed to know just how calculating this girl of my dreams really was.

She also glanced around, then with a smile, she started to open her bloody blouse.

"Thanks," I said, motioning for her to stop. "Always time later."

I really didn't want the reality to change my dreams. It would have never been as good.

She nodded, gave me that smile that scared me to death, started to put herself back together.

She was working on the buttons when I turned suddenly into the police parking lot and hit the horn.

"What are you doing?" she demanded as I drove to the front door of the station, heading for a space that said "Emergency vehicles only."

"Forcing you to do the right thing," I said. "Just tell them what you told me and you'll be fine. You did nothing wrong. You were in shock when you got home and came to me to drive you to the police station because I'm your friend."

Two cops came out of the front door of the station to see what idiot was blaring his horn. I slammed on the brakes, acting as if I had rushed there.

"You're a real bastard," she said.

"Maybe," I said. "But I'm also your only *real* friend. You came to me for help. Now you're getting it."

I shut off the car, took the keys and jumped out.

"Officers," I said. "There's been a tragic accident."

In the passenger seat, the girl I had been afraid of my entire life sat crying.

And I felt free from the terror of that smile, of those eyes, and of that chest.

Especially that chest.

Sometimes facing your fears and staring them down is the best way to conquer them. They just don't seem so large after you do that.

Now Available
from all your favorite booksellers
in trade paper and electronic editions.

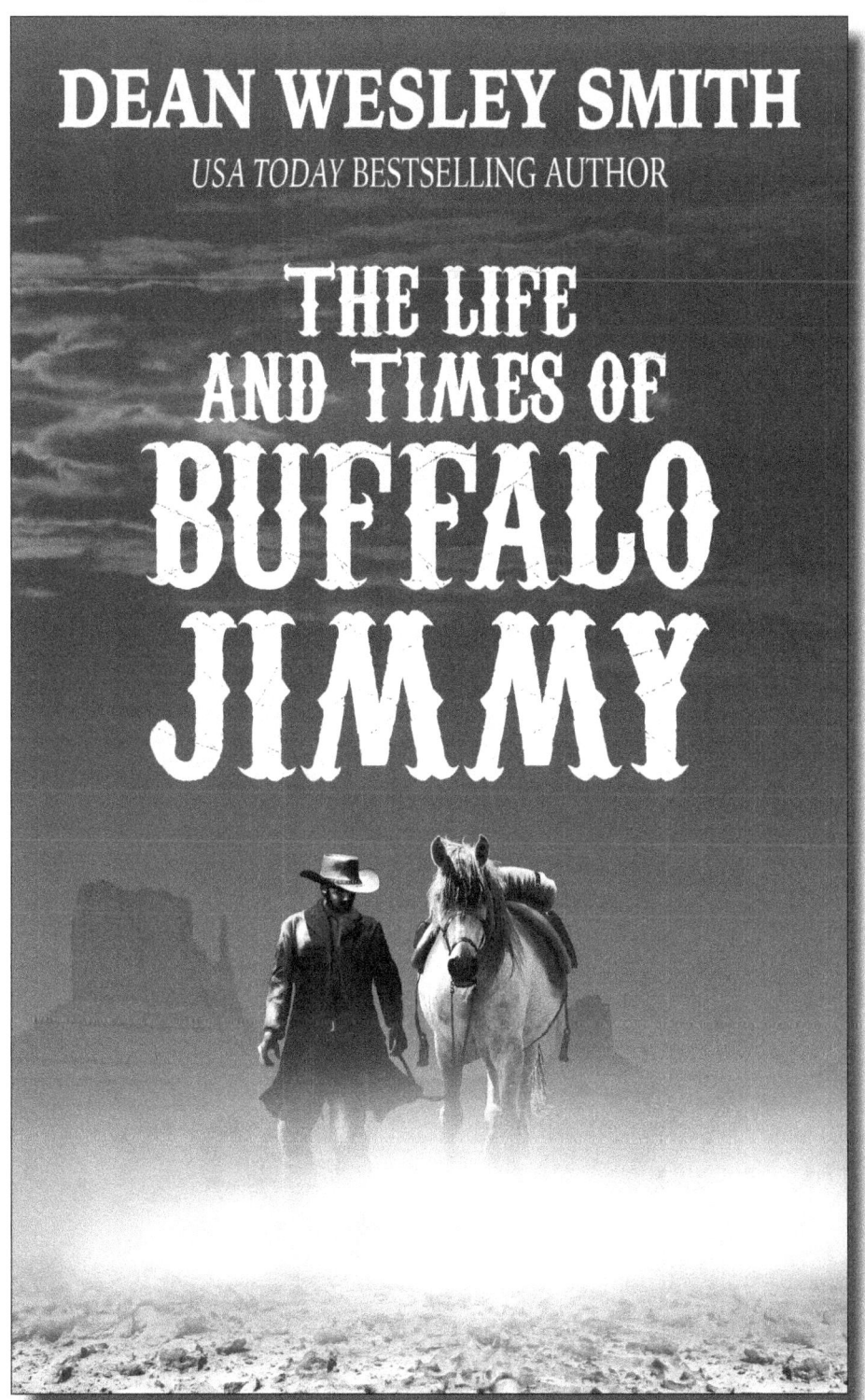

USA TODAY BESTSELLING AUTHOR

DEAN WESLEY
SMITH

STAR MIST

A SEEDERS UNIVERSE NOVEL

A dead alien ship appears close to human space. But in millions of years, no alien race managed to leave its own galaxy.

The alien ship originated in a galaxy over two-hundred-thousand years of travel away. But the Seeders need to know about the alien race, in case they are a threat.

Star Mist takes on the vast scale of the Seeders Universe and expands it even more.

Galaxy-spanning science fiction at its very best.

STAR MIST
A Seeders Universe Novel

For Kris

SECTION ONE
The Beginning Before the Beginning

PROLOGUE

THE ALIEN SHIP looked more like a large pile of black and gray garbage smashed together into a large ball than a spaceship hanging there in the blackness of space just beyond the edge of the Milky Way Galaxy.

Yet Chairman Wade Ray knew it was a ship.

And that ship was the most important discovery in hundreds and hundreds of thousands of years of human history.

Chairman Wade Ray stood, his hands behind his back, in the command center of his ship, staring at the image of the alien ship on the huge monitor that filled one wall of the command center. Ray had his long, silver-gray hair pulled back as always and wore a dark-silk dress shirt and dark slacks and soft leather shoes.

He could feel the tension around him in the huge room like a heavy blanket on a warm night.

Sixteen people manned stations behind him and not a one could be heard. They all felt as he felt, that what they were seeing couldn't be possible.

Tacita, his wife and partner and co-chairman of this ship, stood beside him, also just studying the strange shape of the alien ship. She had her hair extremely short and wore a black silk pantsuit.

To Ray, she was the most beautiful woman he had ever seen and he had been in love with her for more years than he wanted to think about.

He couldn't imagine ever not having her brilliant mind and sharp wit working beside him.

Especially now, when they faced an alien ship.

He shook his head. How was this even possible?

No alien race in thousands and thousands of galaxies had ever managed to survive long enough to build even a galaxy-wide civilization, let alone a ship that could travel the vast distances between galaxies. When the Seeder scout ships discover an alien race growing on any planet in a galaxy, at any level, the Seeders would just go around that galaxy.

Over the centuries, Seeder research ships would watch the alien development, but never interfere. It was one of their most scared laws, learned out of bad experience a long, long time ago.

Very few alien races even survived long enough to make it off their own planet. And even fewer found trans-tunnel drive to jump to other close stars. And for as long as humans had been seeding galaxies with more humans, no alien race had found the refinements to trans-tunnel drives to get the standard speeds to break out of their own limited galaxies.

Yet somehow, he was looking at an alien ship that was between galaxies.

And moving at standard trans-tunnel drive speeds.

"Any life signs at all of any type?" Tacita asked.

"Nothing," Commander Chain said. "We also checked for any form of stasis. Nothing."

Chain was their most trusted second in command on any ship and had been with them thousands of years. He looked, as most Seeders looked, to be about thirty. He had dark brown hair and never was seen out of jeans and a sweatshirt.

"How large is that ship?" Ray asked.

"The size of a Seeder mother ship," Chain said.

Seeder mother ships were the largest ships Seeder's built. Mother ships were the size of small moons and shaped like birds gliding. They could hold a thousand other ships and upwards of a million people comfortably.

"Any equipment at all active?" Tacita asked.

"Except for the trans-tunnel drive still powering it forward," Chain said. "Nothing is active. No atmosphere of any kind, no readings other than the drive. And honestly, it looks like the drive is about to fail as well."

"Can you get a reading on the age?" Ray asked.

"At least two hundred thousand standard years," Chase said. "And from the looks of the damage from impacts of small particles and such after its shields failed, it has been dead for a good hundred thousand of those years."

"Trace back its flight path and put up on the screen where it came from," Tacita said.

Ray was surprised when the image appeared of a thousand galaxies in all their various groupings. Right now they were in the middle of what was called the "Local Cluster" by humans in this galaxy. About thirty galaxies of different sizes and shapes. On the scale on the map on the screen, the local cluster barely showed up as a dot.

The alien ship had originated, or passed through a galaxy that was a vast distance away. Ray guessed there were four hundred galaxies between where it started and where it was now.

"I've accounted for galactic movement on the rough track," Chase said. "That ship never got near another galaxy of any size since it left that galaxy."

"At its speed," Ray asked, "was the ship still functioning when it left that galaxy?"

"Yes," Chase said. "From what we can gather on preliminary scans, it appears it left that galaxy very much alive and functioning."

A dot appeared about halfway along the line of travel on the big screen. "The ship went dead about at this point, from what we can tell so far."

"We need a massive amount of study of this ship," Tacita said. "To find out who this race was and what happened to this ship."

She looked at Ray and he nodded.

Ray agreed completely. They did need a massive amount of study on this ship. And they were going to have to do it carefully and not miss anything.

But his eye went back along the line the ship had taken from that original galaxy. They also needed to know what was happening there and in the galaxies around it.

Two hundred thousand years had passed. Were these aliens expanding as humans did?

And were they warlike?

In space where very, very few advanced civilizations ever emerged from planets, what would the aliens even think if they knew humans were here and spread over hundreds of thousands of galaxies in this area?

Ray kept staring at the image of the ship's path on the wall screen.

Even by the galaxy-spanning scale Seeders worked and thought at, the alien original galaxy was a very, very long distance away.

ONE

ANGIE PARK LET the sounds of her motorcycle die off into the silence of the forest and the ruins around her. Nothing moved, not even a slight breeze among the tall pines and the deserted general store and gas station tucked back into the trees.

The building had been cute at one point in the past, almost like a cottage, but now the paint was peeling, the windows were covered in grime, and weeds were growing thick between the building and the useless gas pump. On one side blackberries were starting to crawl up a wall and in a few years would bury the old building.

She had parked on the edge of the two-lane road that wound up through the

Cascade Mountains. The road in this area had been still in good shape and very few car wrecks had blocked her for the last twenty miles since she had left I-5.

She pulled off her helmet and let her long black hair fall over her shoulders as she dismounted and set the helmet on her leather supply pack. She was thin and tall and had no trouble at all on the large road bikes.

She had a small saddle rifle in a sling on her back and a small caliber gun hidden in a holster on her leg under her jeans.

Her light jacket covered a T-shirt and she unzipped the jacket to let in the fresh mountain air. It was early summer and the heat today was predicted to be around ninety by the middle of the afternoon, even this high in the mountains.

Around her the silence of the Oregon forest seemed to press in, but after all the years of being alone, she was used to silence more than the noise of being around other people. That's why she had volunteered for this task, to go out and tell others about Portland.

Plus she really believed in what Portland was building and wanted everyone to know.

Up a small dirt road in front of her that wound through the tall pine trees, she knew a compound sat at the top of that road with six people living in it. Six survivors of the Event, as it was now being called.

The Event had been a wave of electromagnetic energy that swept over the Earth just over three years ago. It hadn't hurt equipment, but it had killed any exposed humans and dogs and horses and a few other animals. Thankfully it spared cats because she didn't know what she would have done the first few years of being alone without her cats to keep her company.

Humans who had survived were like her. They happened to be underground or in a vault of some type and were protected from the invisible but deadly wave. She had been a Professor of Physics at the University of Oregon and had been three stories down in a lab under the physics department when the Event happened. Millions like her had survived worldwide, and now civilization was working to rebuild.

After the Event, she had moved far up the Columbia Gorge in a home overlooking the river to get away from all the smell of decaying bodies. She had discovered that civilization was rebuilding when convoy after convoy of motorcycles went down the freeway below her home headed for Portland in the spring of the second year. Men, women, and children.

Because of its climate and natural resources, Portland had been picked as one of the five cities to be the center of the new world in this country. She had followed the convoys after a time and saw and listened to what they were doing and trying to build. A month later she had packed up her cats and moved to Portland to try to help.

Now she was doing what they called "outreach" to those who hadn't heard yet about building the new world. It was dangerous, but she had wanted to do it. A couple of her friends had insisted she not go alone, but she had felt that a woman alone would be more convincing than a bunch of people. So far, she had been right about that.

Since so many of the military had survived on ships, submarines, underground compounds, all the top science had survived as well and was being used in the rebuild. She had seen satellite photos of the compound at the end of the dirt road that was her next stop for the day.

She knew that six were living there. They had set up electrical and had running water to most of their buildings and had a pretty decent surveillance system set up that more than likely was watching her now.

That's why she had stopped here, to let them watch her. Last thing she needed to do was surprise anyone who had been surviving and living off of nature for three years. Doing that could get a person really dead really quickly.

Over the years, it seemed that a lot of people had gone completely insane thinking that civilization was gone and that they were left alone.

She had thought at one point she might go insane as well because death was just everywhere. The very reason she had found a place on the top of a hill was for protection from the nut cases roaming around, and to avoid the smell of death that first year. But she had set that home up so she could protect it. Luckily, she never had had to.

She looked up the dirt road that wound into the tall pines. It looked far cooler than where she was standing now near the highway in the sun. She needed to get moving.

She knew the names of four of the six people who were living there. And knew that two of them had surviving family members.

Of the thirty compounds like this one she had approached over the last six months, most had come into the city later on their own terms to see what was going on, and after that, many had moved into town just as she had done.

But others were happy where they were and she respected that.

Her job wasn't to convince them to join humanity again, but to just let them know what was happening.

She took a long cool drink from her canteen, put it back on her bike, then with her hands in the air, started up the road toward the compound. Walking like that told the people watching she knew she was being watched and only wanted to talk.

At least she hoped that's what it told them.

TWO

"OH, NO, ANGIE," Gage Teal said to himself from his apartment living room computer station. "Don't go in there alone. Those folks are whack jobs."

On the screen he saw Angie Park raise her hands above her head and start up the dirt road toward the compound.

"Shit, just shit," Gage said, jamming his feet into his shoes and using his comm link to call his three-member team. She had talked herself out of other tough spots, but from his recon on the people in this compound, there was no talking her way out of this one. The people there were nut jobs and cold-blooded killers.

"Situation," he said to his team when all three answered. "Emergency. Meet me in the staging room in one minute max."

This was what they had all trained for and had done a few times. But his sole person to take care of was Angie Park and right now she was within minutes of being shot.

He finished getting on his shoes and then looked back at the screen. She was almost up the dirt road to the compound.

He had watched her for six months from one of the many shielded Seeder ships in orbit, making sure that she was safe. She was a very special person and the more he had watched her, the more he had come to realize that.

She was special to the Seeders for some reason he didn't know. And she was sometimes foolishly brave. He had fallen for her.

And he had never even met her.

Looked like that was about to change very quickly.

He teleported to the staging room and was the second one there. Only Drake, his second in command for the unit, had arrived ahead of Gage.

Drake looked almost square, with a thick neck and a very wide forehead. He was married to the nicest woman on the planet who was so tiny, Drake could have snapped her in half with his bare hands. Gage didn't want to think about how they had managed two kids.

The staging room was a small room with a wall of weapons that looked like United States military weapons but were actually a bunch more. A large computer screen and a command console filled the other wall.

"Angie?" Drake asked as both of them grabbed their weapons of choice. Both carried what looked like standard issue military rifles and both strapped another gun on their hips in a holster. The rifles were actually laser and could kill or stun a person from a half mile away.

"She's about to walk into a mess," Gage said, pulling up the large screen as Jean Marsh and Rollie King appeared and moved to the gun wall. They were a couple and looked like twins instead of being married. Both were as tall as Gage at six foot, both wore body-shirts that made their intense muscle training show clearly. Both wore their brown hair short and only Marsh pretended to break the mold with an earring on one ear.

But they loved to dress exactly the same to mess with people's minds at times. Clearly they had just come directly from a workout.

"What's Angie's walking into this time?" Drake asked.

They had jumped for Angie three times before and hadn't had to show themselves. But this time was bad, real bad.

Gage showed them the compound and the six people as they gathered around the big screen.

One person was staying in a cabin with a rifle, one was getting set as a sniper in a tree near the road, and the other three were waiting for Angie to come to them.

A sixth man had already gone down to the road and taken Angie's motorcycle and was pushing it up the dirt road.

"She's in deep this time," Marsh said, shaking her head.

"We stun and relocate," Gage said. "I'll clear the sniper and the guy with the bike, Marsh and King, you two take the three that will face Angie on the road. Drake, you take the one in the cabin. Wait for my mark."

All three of them nodded and each pointed to a spot they would jump to.

"Let's get into positions," Gage said.

Then he touched a key on the command table and said, "Four transporting to the surface."

"Clear," the answer came back.

They all teleported at once and a moment later Gage found himself in a small hidden area behind Angie where he could see the sniper and hear the conversation Angie was about to have.

The air felt warm, almost hot, and the smell of pine filled the air.

As he got ready and made sure his rifle was on stun, his team checked in that they were in position.

Now Available
from all your favorite booksellers
in trade paper and electronic editions.

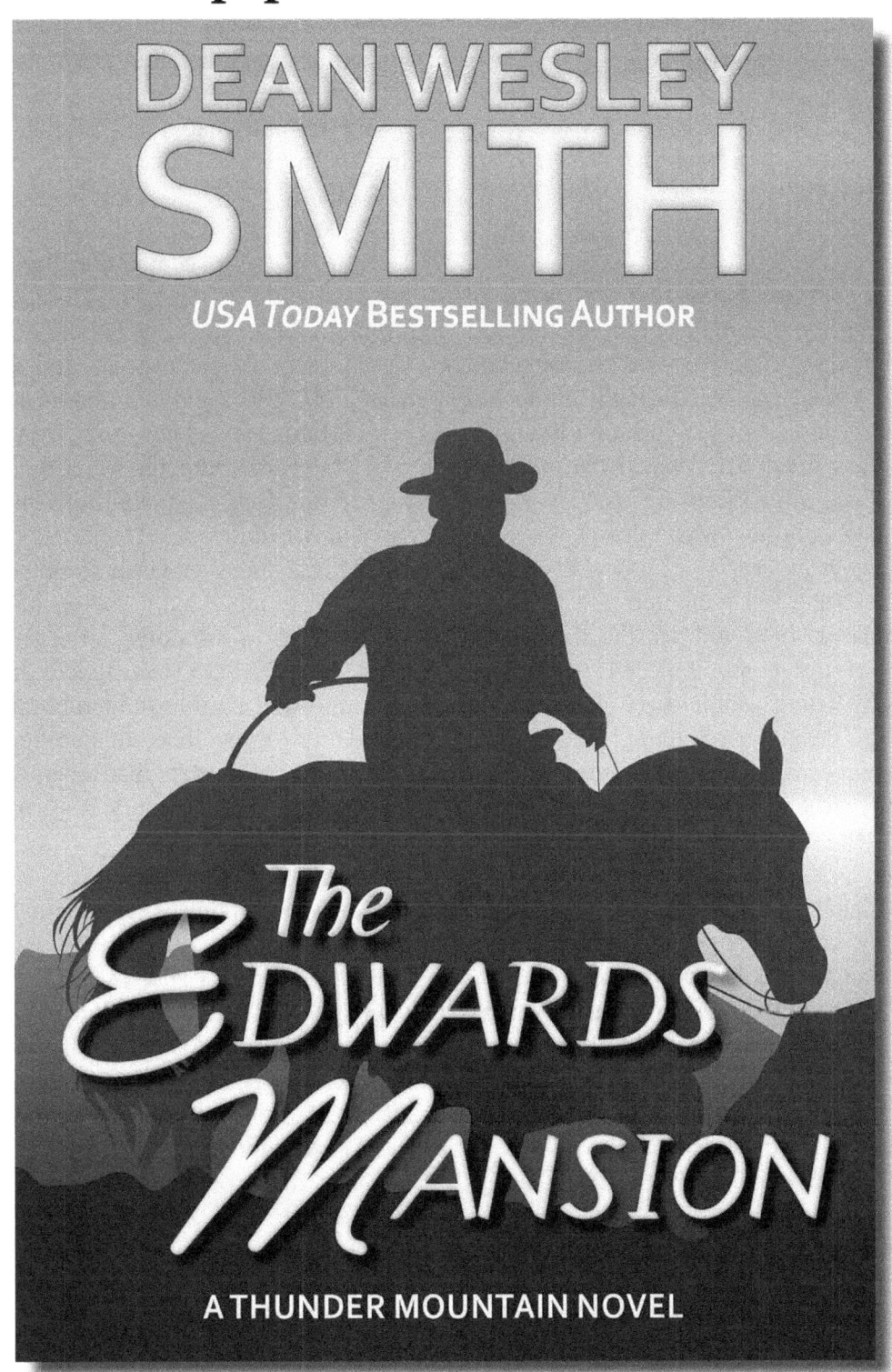

This wasn't the way he had hoped to meet Angie. But it looked like it was going to have to do.

If something didn't go wrong and she got killed. He would never forgive himself if that happened.

THREE

IT TOOK HER seven minutes to walk up the dirt road before she crested over a slight ridge. She was sweating and now wished she had brought along her canteen instead of leaving it on the bike. It wasn't much after ten in the morning and it was already getting hot.

And walking with her hands in the air was never an easy task, especially going uphill as she had been doing.

Ahead she could see the five buildings of the compound, all well-maintained. Three single-story houses and two tall-peaked barns sat in a cluster with some fenced-in chicken areas to one side. The fence on those were tall and strung between solid poles, more than likely in an attempt to keep out mountain lions that roamed these hills.

She kept her hands in the air and kept walking toward the compound.

After another hundred paces, a man and two women stepped out of one house and moved to meet her. All three carried rifles, but had them cradled in their arms or down in one hand.

The woman on the right Angie recognized as Bettie Collins from photos. The woman on the left was her sister LeAnne. They had both lived in a small town to the east of here. She had no idea how they survived the Event. They must have been in a deep basement or something at the time as Angie had been.

The tall, very thin man in the middle Angie didn't recognize, but he looked to be about her age at thirty and had intelligence in his eyes that didn't seem to miss anything.

She instantly had a bad feeling about him.

Instantly.

That was unusual.

None of them seemed at all worried about meeting a stranger. That wasn't normal in these situations either.

All three of them were dressed in jeans, light shirts, and work boots and all their clothing looked new and clean.

As they got within ten steps, the three stopped and Bettie signaled for Angie to stop and she did.

She was about ten yards from the tree line and very much out in the open.

"Put your arms down," Bettie said. "That had to be hard walking like that."

Angie did, smiling and rubbing her shoulders. "I've done it numbers of times, but it never gets that much easier. I'm Angela Park, but everyone just calls me Angie."

"Everyone," the man asked, clearly puzzled and not introducing himself at all.

Angie nodded. "That's what I'm here to tell you about. Civilization is slowly rebuilding. Portland is one of the five cities picked to be one of the centers. I'm just out trying to inform everyone about what is happening."

"How many people are in Portland?" Bettie asked.

Angie shrugged. "Last count about forty thousand."

"Forty thousand," LeAnne said, breathlessly.

The man didn't even flinch.

Angie nodded. "And your Aunt Carol is there and knew I was coming out this way and told me to send her best wishes. She survived as well."

Angie thought both Bettie and LeAnne were going to collapse right there, but both managed to take deep breaths and then look at each other.

Angie was starting to feel that something was off here. She wasn't sure, but her little voice was starting to get worried. These people were not reacting in the way that survivors on their own normally reacted, which was usually with fear and then relief that civilization was rebuilding.

"Since civilization destroyed itself one time," the man said, "why is everyone so fired up to rebuild?"

"Humans had nothing to do with the Event," Angie said. "It was an electromagnetic wave that came out of deep space and swept over the entire planet. The scientists who knew it was coming thought it would be harmless. Turns out it was at a certain frequency that fried something in our human brains and everyone who wasn't either underground or protected behind steel died instantly and painlessly. It did not harm equipment."

"How do you know all this?" he asked.

"May I?" she asked, pointing to her back pocket.

He nodded and didn't raise his rifle.

He should have raised his rifle.

Something was very off.

As she pulled out three folded sheets and offered them to him, she glanced around looking for the three others who lived here to be in positions to kill her at the guy's signal. If they wanted to, she was as good as dead. She was a good ten running steps from the nearest shelter.

Bettie stepped forward and took the sheets, then stepped back and looked at the papers, handing them to the others one at a time.

"That information was recorded from the International Space Station," Angie said, staying on her practiced patter. "We finally got the men who were up there down a year ago, and used a couple existing rockets to resupply them in the meantime."

All three looked at each sheet. LeAnne held onto them when they were finished.

They had no questions at all.

Under normal circumstances, they would have questions. A lot of questions.

What the hell was going on here?

Angie took a deep breath and kept going. "The third sheet is a summary of what is happening in Portland and around the world, when the first major election will be for both Portland and the United States. And so on."

"Seems very civilized like," the man said.

Again Angie pointed to her pocket. "May I?"

The man nodded and Angie pulled out an iPhone and charging cord and a paper list and offered them.

Bettie again stepped forward and took the iPhone, charging cord, and paper.

Then she stepped back beside the man.

No comment about how useless it was, nothing. More than anything Angie wanted to just turn and run, but more than likely if she did that she would be cut down from the hidden guns of the others.

"Cell towers are now working along the Interstate Five route from Portland down to Eugene and all around the

Portland area," Angie said. "That's a list of numbers you can call for more information if you go down near the freeway. And your aunt's number is on there as well."

Nothing.

Not one bit of comment at all.

Angie had every alarm bell in her body going off. She had to get out of there and get going now!

She smiled. "Nice chatting with all of you. I hope you decide to stop into the city when you get a chance. It's very nice."

She raised her hands and stepped backwards.

"I don't think you'll be leaving just yet," the man said, bringing his rifle up and aiming at her.

LeAnne and Bettie did the same.

Behind her, she heard a man huffing. She glanced over her shoulder to see a man pushing her bike up the road. "This is a nice ride," he said as he got over the crest of the small rise.

"What's going on here?" she asked.

"We never allow visitors to leave once they know we are here," the man said.

"We have to protect ourselves," Bettie said.

"We are so sorry," LeAnne said.

But to Angie she didn't look sorry at all. More than likely numbers of people had stumbled into this place and were buried in back somewhere, which is where she was about to end up.

Why had she ever thought she could do this job alone?

FOUR

GAGE LISTENED to the conversation Angie was having with the three and then the stunned and worried sound of her voice when the guy with her bike came up behind her.

"Stand ready," Gage said to his team through their comm links. "And Marsh and King, back me on the guy with the bike in case I can't get a clear shot."

"Copy," Marsh said.

He watched Angie stand there, facing almost certain death, staying calm and proud. She was an amazing woman and when this was over, it was time he finally got to know her.

He had an apartment in Portland to be part of the team there when needed. In fact, all of them did. And each of them protected a certain Seeder-important person in town. In fact, if his team ever took a name, it would be Guardian Angels.

Marsh and King were assigned to watch over a couple by the name of Carrie Noack and Matt Ladel. They had actually become friends with them without ever telling Carrie or Matt that they were being guarded. And Carrie and Matt didn't know about the Seeders ships in orbit or the vast human society that covered the galaxy and far beyond.

But for some reason, those higher in the Seeders considered Carrie and Matt worth protecting, along with Angie, who didn't know about the Seeders either.

Drake had been assigned to watch and protect Benny Slade. Benny and his girlfriend were already Seeders, but they had elected to remain on the planet and unknown to Benny and his girlfriend, Drake was watching out for them.

The team had not had to be called for a problem with anyone but Angie. Gage had a hunch that Angie wouldn't stop doing her job until someone told her about the Seeders. And Gage had no idea when that would be.

So he stood ready to take out the sniper from the tree and the guy with her motorcycle the moment it looked like Angie's talking could no longer save the day.

She was one brave person, going out and doing this alone. Wow.

FIVE

I AM NO threat to you," Angie said. "All we wanted to do was tell you about what was happening. You are free to stay here for the rest of your lives. No one cares."

"Someone always cares," the man said.

The two women nodded. Both of them looked very pained. Clearly the year after the Event had not gone well for them.

The man pushing the bike had stopped behind her about ten steps right at the tree line. She had no doubt, without looking, that he had a gun trained on her as well.

If these people were so worried about being found, maybe Angie had one last thing to say to save her life.

"If you allow me to leave here," Angie said, "I will just cross this compound off as not interested."

"I am sure you would," the man said.

"But if you kill me, if anything happens to me, the new government will come swooping in here faster than you can ever imagine. Murder is still murder in a civilized world."

"No one knows where you are at," the man said, laughing. "You're just like those religious types who used to bang on doors back when the world was still alive. You just want us to follow you to your church so you can take our things."

"Check the bag on my bike," Angie said, staring at the man. "There are satellite images of this compound that were taken just recently. They are watching us now as I speak because they knew I was going to be here. You think I am stupid enough to walk in here alone?"

She was damn proud of herself that her voice didn't shake when she said that, even though she had been just as stupid as she claimed not to be.

The man nodded and behind Angie she could hear the other guy rummaging in her pack. He pulled out the photos of this compound and let out a small gasp. Then he let the bike drop and moved around Angie to hand the images to the man between LeAnne and Bettie.

The man looked at them and suddenly didn't seem so sure of himself.

"So go ahead and shoot me," Angie said. "But expect the helicopters and police to descend on this compound in less than two hours. But you let me go, I just cross this place off as you not being interested and you can go on with your lives for as long as you want."

"I think you are bluffing," the man said.

"Look at the photo," she said, actually bluffing her socks off. "Can you tell when it was taken? I left Portland two days ago with it. They took it for me so I would know what they were watching and so I could find this place easily. You are my third stop. They watch me closely at every stop."

The man looked at the photo, then simply tore it up and dropped it on the ground.

"We let you leave and for sure you tell everyone about us. We kill you and take the chance that you weren't being watched. I think we'll go with that second chance."

He raised his gun and at that moment all four of them just slumped to the ground. And there was a crashing beside the road and another woman slumped out of a tree and fell to the ground.

What the hell was going on?

She stood there staring at the four bodies in front of her, letting her racing heart slow just a little. She had been seconds away from being very dead.

Very, very dead.

What had happened?

At that moment, a man came walking up the road, smiling at her. "Bet you thought you were bluffing, didn't you?"

She opened her mouth to say something, then just shut it.

The guy walking toward her had a smile that lit up his face and a body that would turn any head. He looked to be about six-feet tall, with wide shoulders and short, dark hair. His skin looked smooth and tan, as if he spent a lot of time in the sun. He wore jeans, a dark green T-shirt, and had a gun on his hip in a holster that just looked like it belonged there.

"Angie, sorry we had to finally meet like this," he said, extending his hand.

She took his calm, dry hand in her sweaty hand and shook it, still stunned beyond words as to what had happened.

"I'm Lieutenant Gage Teal. Former United States Special Forces. I've been in charge of your protection detail for the last six months."

"Holy shit," she said, almost gasping for air. "You just saved my life."

"And that's exactly why we have been watching you all along," he said, smiling. "Me and my team always went in ahead of your scheduled stop to make sure you got the protection you needed."

"Thank you," she said, not really knowing what to think other than that she was still alive and the man responsible could be a Greek God. Wearing a damn T-shirt that showed muscles no human should ever have.

"I thought you were going to talk your way out of this mess as well," he said. "You had the nutball thinking there for a while."

She laughed. "Desperation brings on wild stories. I just didn't know any of them were true."

"Ninety-nine percent of the time," he said, "it is better to think you are alone when facing these survivors. Glad we were here for that one percent."

"Yeah," Angie said, "me, too." She was still trying to catch her breath. Near-death experiences can make you real short of breath it seemed.

"Can you help me get these people rounded up? My men have spread out to scout the area to make sure no one else is around."

"Are they dead?" Angie asked. "And what kind of weapon was that?"

"A ray guy, actually," he said, laughing "sort of along the same principle as the wave that killed in the Event, only not fatal. Just knocks a person out for a few hours and gives them a real nasty headache."

"Good," she said, laughing.

"The fifth one fell out of a tree over here where we stunned her," he said, moving off to the right.

They each took one of the woman's arms and dragged her back to the others in the middle of the road. She was about Angie's age—around thirty—and also looked as clean and fresh as the others. But clearly the Event and this leader guy had really twisted their minds and made them into killers.

"Where is the sixth one?" she asked after they got the woman near the others.

"In the big house," he said. "We can leave her there for the pickup."

"What are you going to do with them?" she asked.

"Helicopter will take them down into the old Central America and dump them off with enough water and food to survive for a few days. It's pretty wild down there still. Perfect for their type. What they manage to do from there is their business."

She laughed. "I love that. Serves the creeps right."

He walked her back to her bike and helped her get it upright again. Her helmet must still be down near the highway.

She secured her bag on her bike and then turned to look at him. Damn, he had green eyes.

She loved green eyes.

Now she wasn't sure if her heart was still racing from almost being killed or racing because the man standing next to her was so damn good-looking.

How was it possible that the man who had saved her ass was handsome and had green eyes?

"How about from now on out we do this as a team?" she asked.

"We have been a team since you went out the first time," he said, smiling. "You just didn't know it."

"How about you and I work together then, so I know your plans and I don't go off course and change plans on you and get myself killed in some place you can't rescue my skinny ass?"

He laughed. "I like that a lot. So what are your plans next?"

"I'm going back to Portland to my wonderful house and my two cats, take a long, cool bath, and try to stop shaking."

He nodded, the smile still on his face.

"After that I am going to go out and have a nice dinner at a nice restaurant and a few drinks to try to bury the memory of these nut cases."

"Would you like company for dinner and a few drinks?" he asked.

"I would love that," she said. "Do you know where I live?"

She wasn't sure that she wanted to know the answer to that, but she had asked anyway.

"Not a clue," he said.

"Northwest sector of town," she said. "You ever heard of a restaurant called Danny's in the Pearl area?"

Some Classic Dean Wesley Smith Stories
Available at your favorite booksellers.

"Best chicken and pizza in all of Portland," he said, his smile lighting up an already hot and bright day.

"Six p.m.," she said, climbing on her bike and firing it up.

"Six p.m.," he said, nodding to her.

She turned her bike and headed slowly down the dirt road, not daring to look at the lieutenant behind her.

She had almost died, been rescued by the most handsome man left on the planet, and now she had a date with him.

If he had come in on a white horse it wouldn't have made it any stranger, other than the fact that horses had been killed in the Event as well.

Who knew that facing down crazy survivalists could get her a date.

It was a strange damn world, of that there was no doubt.

And she was going to enjoy every minute of still being alive, and maybe later, every inch of the body of the man who saved her.

A girl could hope.

SIX

"GOT A DATE, huh?" Drake said as he came around the end of the house dragging the woman who had been inside through the dust like she was so much luggage.

"Figured it was the best way," Gage said, smiling, really, really happy that Angie had said yes to meeting him.

"So we were scouting, huh?" Marsh said, appearing out of the tree line twenty steps to the right. King appeared at the same time on the left.

"Easier to just let her get on the road again," Gage said.

"Sure, sure," Marsh said, shaking her head.

Drake dropped the unconscious woman in the pile of other human garbage. "So what exactly are we doing with these sickos?"

"I'll have transport drop them with some supplies on a beach in Central America a very long distance from any other humans. Not my issue if they survive or not, but they will be alone like they wanted. They just won't have anyone but each other to kill."

"Perfect," Drake said.

"Call us if you need backup on this date," Marsh said, smiling at Gage.

"Don't call me," Drake said. "My wife and I are having dinner with my charges tonight in Portland. We're going to tell them we are Seeders as well."

"But not that you have been guarding them?" Gage asked, surprised.

"Nope," Drake said. "We like them as friends and just figured we could expand the menu for meals some if they knew who we really were."

Gage laughed. "Real good point."

"Wish we could tell Carrie and Matt," Marsh said. "We like them as well."

"I have a hunch the reason we are all doing this guarding will come clear sooner rather than later," Gage said.

"You know something we don't?" Marsh asked.

"Just a gut sense," Gage said. "When I report how close Angie came to being killed today, movement might just happen."

"Yeah," Drake said. "Real good point. Now can we get out of this heat?"

With that, Gage touched his ear. "Four transporting on board."

"Clear," came the response.

And a moment later they were back putting their weapons away. Gage jumped back to his apartment after thanking his team and wrote his report and submitted it.

Then he headed for the shower, whistling, after spending an hour watching Angie ride into Portland to make sure that she got safely to her apartment.

He had a date with a beautiful and courageous woman. It didn't get any better than that.

SEVEN

ANGIE LAY IN her tub in her wonderful apartment, just letting the water calm her and take away the shaking.

Well, at least attempt to take away the shaking. She had never had this kind of reaction before to an event. But she had never gotten within a second of sure death before either.

When she got home, she had forced herself to make a sandwich and eat it before taking a bath. The food and the warm water were helping, but still every time she thought about how close she had come to dying today, she started shaking again.

She was getting annoyed at it and also annoyed that her shaking was making water slosh out of the tub.

Finally, she drained the water and took a very cold shower and then washed her long black hair. The day was warm enough it would dry before her dinner date.

And doing such a regular thing and the cold water finally got the shakes stopped.

She couldn't believe that a handsome man had just shown up, saved her life, and then arranged to have a date with her. That was a very, very goofy thing.

Except for the part that he had saved her life.

And that he was scary handsome.

All she really wanted to do was touch those muscles under his T-shirt to see if they were for real. He looked to be about her age at thirty, but she had never met a man in that kind of shape at that age before. Clearly they existed.

What she didn't realize was that those stun weapons they had used existed. Especially done in a way so that they

looked like regular-issue rifles. That seemed pretty advanced, especially only three years after the Event.

There was an awful lot about the handsome stranger who had saved her life that she wanted to know.

She checked the time. She needed to get dressed and get going on the four-block walk down to the restaurant.

This would be a very interesting dinner. Not only because he was so handsome and had green eyes and muscles that wouldn't stop, but because she wanted to know exactly how he had followed her for six months without her knowing it.

And where those stun weapons came from.

And if he had a girlfriend.

EIGHT

CHAIRMAN SOMA asked Gage to report to his office at once just forty minutes before he was to transport to the planet for the date with Angie.

Gage and his team were stationed on the Seeders ship *Home Stand* that was one of five shielded ships in orbit over this planet to try to help it rebuild from a devastating hit by an electromagnetic wave. Thousands of Seeders were implanted in communities around the globe to help in the rebuilding.

But in almost a year being on this ship, Gage had not had a chance to meet Chairman Soma.

Every Seeder ship was its own business that worked to make a profit and continue, thus what would be called the captain was called the chairman. Gage knew what he was getting for his guard

duty was very high pay, so for some reason this planet out of all the other human planets in this galaxy was special.

You didn't often see five Seeder ships in orbit around any planet for any reason, especially planets that hadn't advanced far enough yet to join the larger group of planets.

Gage had a hunch his report today was what caused this sudden meeting with the chairman.

Gage finished putting on his tennis shoes and transported to the chairman's office.

The room was huge, with a large oak-colored wooden desk, soft brown carpet, pictures of various planets and star-groups on the walls in oranges and reds. There was a large brown cloth couch and a few large chairs that matched.

The room felt comfortable and lived-in.

As he arrived, Chairman Soma stood from one of the chairs and extended his hand. "Great job today keeping Angie Park alive."

"That's what I am assigned to do," Gage said.

Captain Soma was a solid man, with huge shoulders and no gut at all. He looked like he could pick a couch up off the floor with one hand. He had short-cut brown hair and dark, penetrating eyes. He wore what looked like sweat pants and a massive body shirt and no shoes.

Another man stood from a second chair. The other man was tall and had very long silver hair. He wore a silk shirt and dark pants and just radiated power and intelligence.

Soma turned and said, "Gage Teal, I would like you to meet Chairman Wade Ray."

Gage shook his hand and said, "Nice meeting you."

"Actually," Ray said, "the pleasure is mine."

Then Gage's brain kicked in and he realized who he had just met was the legend of all Seeders, maybe the oldest human alive. He was rumored to be hundreds of thousands of years old.

Gage started to open his mouth to say something but not a damn thought came to his mind to say.

The two chairmen indicated that Gage should take a seat on the couch and he did.

Chairman Ray got right to the point. "We think it's time to bring in Angie Park and tell her about us."

Of all the things either of these men could have said, that was the biggest surprise. And it finally explained why he and his team had been guarding her for all this time.

"She has Seeder genes?"

Both men nodded.

"She is very special," Ray said, "and so are you and four others in this area of this planet."

Again Gage opened his mouth to say something, but then realized that the greatest human to have ever lived had just called him special.

Ray just smiled as Gage managed to get some sort of sense of thought back in control. Ray would not be here if there wasn't a need for some mission and since he had just called him special along with the others on the surface, that meant that whatever quality they all had was needed for something very important.

He had been around the military part of the Seeders for a few hundred years now and he knew that was how it worked.

"I assume you have a mission for us," Gage said, "meaning me and the other five still on the planet. And whatever makes us special is the key to this mission."

Ray glanced at Soma who just smiled and shook his head.

"We do," Ray said. "And yes, you are correct. But if you wouldn't mind, I would like to explain it all to everyone at the same time."

Gage understood that completely and nodded. "So what do you need me to do?"

"You know Angie Park as well as anyone, since you have been tracking her," Ray said. "Figure out a way to introduce the fact that this ship is here and what Seeders actually are."

Gage nodded. "I have a date with her in exactly ten minutes. How long do I have?"

"As soon as possible," Ray said. "A few days at most."

"And the others I assume are the ones my team has also been protecting?"

"They are," Ray said. "Two are already Seeders and will be bringing along the other two."

"What about my team?" Gage asked.

"They will be going with you on your mission if you want them, and they agree to it, as you must do as well."

Gage nodded and stood.

The other two men stood and both shook his hand.

Chairman Soma said, "Report to me your progress and I will keep Chairman Ray updated."

"And enjoy the date," Ray said, smiling.

"I will," Gage said and then jumped back to his apartment on the ship, splashed some water on his face to try to get his mind working, and then told command that he was jumping to the planet.

"Clear," the command voice came back.

A moment later he jumped to a sidewalk near the restaurant. He was shielded so no one could see him and then, as he walked down the street, he dropped the shield.

The evening was a beautiful summer evening in what used to be called the Rose City. The air had a freshness to it and a slight breeze kept the air comfortable. In this area of town a number of cafes had tables and chairs outside on the sidewalk and they were filled with people talking and laughing.

One thing for sure about surviving something like the Event, it made the people of this planet very cheerful and looking to enjoy life. All of them had lost loved ones and family and knew they were lucky to be alive and rebuilding.

He had a date with a beautiful woman. One of the smartest and bravest women he had ever had the chance to meet. It had been a very long time for him, maybe almost eighty years since he and his first and so far only wife had decided to go their own ways. They still loved each other, but just had very different interests.

He had a few one-night stands out of bars over the years, but his job kept him busy and not really meeting the right kind of women.

He had a hunch Angie was the right kind of woman now that she was being recruited to be a Seeder.

If he didn't blow this.

And why he and Angie were special to someone like Chairman Wade Ray was beyond him.

In all his life he had never been this confused about anything.

And excited at the same time that he could be honest with Angie Park.

He just had to hope she didn't end up hating him for being an alien.

A human alien, but still an alien.

NINE

ANGIE STOOD just outside the restaurant watching for Gage Teal. There was no chance in hell she was going to go inside, get a table, and then sit there alone if he stood her up.

Or if she had just been imagining all that this afternoon.

The evening was flat perfect, with a cool breeze off the river and the temperature in the mid-seventies. She had decided to just go with her normal way of dressing in jeans, but had put on her best new blue blouse and some pearl earrings that had been her mother's.

Angie felt dressed up. And that was all that mattered.

Then suddenly there he was, walking toward her down the sidewalk. He also had on jeans, tennis shoes, and a white dress shirt with the sleeves rolled up. He saw her and broke into the same smile she had seen up in the mountains earlier after he had saved her life.

And that smile almost melted her right there on the sidewalk.

"Sorry I am slightly late," he said as he came up to her. "A meeting with some top brass."

"Only just got here myself," she said, smiling back at him and those intense green eyes.

God, if she wasn't careful, she might just stare into those eyes all night and not say a word.

"Hungry?" he asked, indicating the restaurant they were in front of that smelled wonderful.

The smell was a mixture of garlic and pasta and fresh-baked bread. This place was also known for the best pizza in town and chicken in an Italian sauce that could melt in a person's mouth. After getting here, the smell of garlic and pizza had made her decide that was what she was going to have.

"Famished," she said. "Almost being killed can do that for a girl."

He laughed as she turned to lead the way inside and damn if she didn't love the sound of his laugh as well.

It was going to be everything she could do to just not jump him right here in the restaurant. She realized this afternoon that she hadn't had a date since the Event. For some reason she had just never met a person she wanted to date amid all the death. But now that life was returning to at least Portland and a few other cities around the world, she was beyond ready.

Also during the first part of the last few years, her focus had been on staying alive and then helping in the recovery. But she had never been the celibate type before the Event. While working on her Doctorate in Physics, she had even been engaged. But they had both been too busy and that had broken off.

And after she became a professor, all the men just looked too young for her, even though she wasn't much older than most of them.

Of course, even when she was dating, she just knew she sucked at long-term relationships. Just sucked.

But now she had a date and if she didn't screw this up, it might be something worthwhile for some great sex for a few months.

They managed to get a table in the back corner of the restaurant. The table was wood with a red tablecloth on it and the chairs were solid and also wood. A couple tall plants divided their table from the nearest one and gave them some privacy, which she liked.

A waiter named Bud took their drink order and left them staring at each other.

"I am so glad I finally get a chance to meet and talk with you," Gage said.

"I'm glad you and I can talk as well," she said, smiling at him. "If you hadn't been shadowing me this morning I wouldn't be here."

He just shrugged, which she loved. "Just doing my job."

"And who hired you to do this job?" she asked. "And why me?"

"Honestly," he said, "those are the two toughest questions you could have asked and I will tell you the truth on both a little later, except I honestly don't know why you."

Then she watched as he laughed. "And to be honest, I don't know why me and my team either. So I'm hoping together we can get some answers as to why both of us ended up in that compound this morning."

She frowned. She had not expected that kind of answer at all. She wasn't sure what she had been expecting, but it wasn't that.

"How about we get to know each other a little first," he asked. "What did you do before the Event? Were you married or engaged and if either of those questions are too personal, tell me to mind my own business."

She laughed and the worry in his eyes dropped away.

"You sure you want to know?" she asked.

"Very much," he said, nodding.

"Not married and no boyfriend before the Event and I was a professor of physics."

He sat back with that, clearly thinking for a moment. Then he said, "That's cool."

"That I didn't have a boyfriend?" she asked, smiling at him and he laughed.

"No, the physics part," he said, "but glad you didn't lose a loved one as well."

She looked into those green eyes. Did she really want to know this man's background or not. Finally she decided she did. "And you?"

"Pretty close to your expertise, actually," he said. "I have a doctorate in mathematics."

That rocked her back. God, he was smart and handsome.

Holy shit.

"In fact," he said, "all four members of my team have higher degrees in one thing or another."

She shook her head and he laughed.

"Military image doesn't often cover higher degrees, does it? Does that make you want to stop this dinner?"

She laughed and said, "Oh, I think I can put up with someone who is smart for at least the length of a dinner. So that education scares off women, does it?"

He shrugged and took a piece of bread from a basket that had just been dropped on the table by a waiter. "Honestly, been so long since I went out to dinner with anyone but friends, I don't remember. Never was much good at long-term stuff."

She loved the sound of that. He was in the same place with relationships she was in.

Maybe, if she didn't say something really stupid, there was hope for this after all.

At least short-term hope, and right now, in this new world, that was all she wanted.

TEN

SIX WONDERFUL HOURS later, they both came up for air after a second passionate love-making session at her apartment.

They were in her big king bed on top of wonderful-feeling cloth sheets. The city lights around them lit up the room that she had made very much her own with a few stuffed animals a couple dressers covered with knicknacks, and cat toys.

He had fallen instantly for her two cats who seemed to think he was the best thing ever, thankfully.

Gage couldn't believe how much he enjoyed every moment with Angie, and just touching her had sent shivers through him the first time, as if making a connection he had been waiting his entire life to make.

Even though he had to be careful with some things he said during dinner and on the wonderful, hand-in-hand walk to her apartment, he hadn't enjoyed time with anyone else like that before.

She rested beside him now, trying to catch her breath, her beautiful body wonderful in the lights through the window. She didn't seem to be even in the slightest bit modest in front of him, which he also loved.

Finally, she rolled over to face him. "Where the hell did you come from?"

He laughed. "You honestly don't want to know."

She moved in to kiss him, then pulled back. "How about from this moment forward no more secrets ever from each other."

He looked deep into her wonderful eyes and then nodded. "Deal. No more secrets."

He had to do this, so he might as well start now.

"So where are you from?" she asked.

"If I'm going to tell you the truth," he said, "I first have to show you something."

"Do I have to get dressed?" she asked, smiling at him, "or is this something more intimate?"

"I think getting dressed might be a really good idea," he said, laughing and then kissing her hard. "I want to show you my place."

He loved kissing her more than he even wanted to admit to himself.

"Oh, bummer," she said. "She rolled off the bed and headed to the bathroom.

"Trust me," he said, "seeing my apartment will be worth it."

"It had better be," she said as she disappeared.

He laughed. She had no idea at all what was coming.

Ten minutes later they were both dressed and standing in the middle of her living room near the front door. The main room of her apartment was amazingly comfortable, with books scattered all over the place, a couple of nice quilts on a large chair and a tan couch, and a wall full of books.

He had never allowed himself to spy on her in this apartment, so this had been a pleasant surprise. He only followed her when she left.

He took her hand and looked into her wonderful brown eyes and smiling face. "What you are about to experience will be a shock, but please keep that brilliant mind of yours open and together we'll get through this to the other side."

She frowned. "What's in this apartment of yours?"

"A lot of books and some computer equipment, just like here, only nowhere near as nice and no cats, sadly," he said.

Then he squeezed her hand and touched his ear and said, "Two to come aboard."

"Clear."

The next moment he had transported the two of them to his apartment.

He thought her grip on his hand might break it as she looked around.

"What the hell just happened? And what are we aboard? And how?"

He could hear the panic in her voice.

"This is my apartment," he said, waving his arms around. "You asked me where I am from, this is it for the moment, but now let me answer your real question as to where I am from."

Without giving her a chance to ask a question, he jumped them both to an observatory lounge.

It was empty except for a few folding chairs. The room was large enough to hold banquets in it and one entire wall was clear and looked out over the Earth below.

He could feel her starting to get faint and he instantly helped her sit in a chair and pulled up another beside her, slightly facing her as she stared out at the planet Earth below.

Then she shook her head and looked around and then back at the fantastic view of the planet below. Then she said, "I thought it had all been a dream."

"Excuse me?" he asked.

"I was in a room like this one a number of days after the Event," she said, looking at him. "It was crowded with all of us from the surface and it smelled of death. The fine people on the ship were trying to give us help and food. They said they got us out of the way of a second electromagnetic pulse and then would put us back, but most of us would never remember. I remembered."

"Oh, my," he said. He was more stunned than he wanted to admit. He had expected she would be in panic and it would take help to calm her down.

She turned and looked at him. "So it wasn't a dream? That actually happened?"

He nodded. "It was a massive rescue operation from a thousand planets in this galaxy to save as many after the first Event as they could. From my understanding, they saved everyone who was alive from the second wave."

She nodded. "That's what they said. I remember clearly."

She went back to looking at the Earth below and they sat silently for a few minutes. He was doing his best to try to figure out the next step.

Then she turned to him and said, "You promised to tell me where you are from."

He pointed off to the right and said, "I was born four hundred and ten years ago on a planet much like the one below orbiting a sun in a small cluster galaxy that is a satellite galaxy to the Milky Way."

She blinked, then said, "I always knew I liked older men."

It took him a moment, then he laughed.

And she smiled, which was something he hadn't expected this soon.

ELEVEN

"SO EXPLAIN all this," she said, sweeping her arm around at the large banquet room with a wall that had a view to die for of Earth below. "Start by telling me what this ship is all about."

She needed some answers and she needed them quickly before she started making up stuff she didn't want to think about. And she could feel a lot of anger just boiling below the surface.

"The name of this ship is the *Home Stand*," Gage said. "From my understanding, about three-hundred-thousand people live and work on this ship."

"Wow," she said, stunned. "Bigger than most cities."

"It is huge," he said. "I've been on board for under a year and haven't even seen a tiny fraction of it."

"And what's it doing here?" she asked, trying to keep her mind focused on getting answers one at a time before she totally went crazy.

"It's one of five Seeder ships that are stationed here to try to help your planet recover from the Event. All are shielded from any kind of detection. No one in any of your forming governments knows anything about the ships here helping."

"Seeders?" she asked.

"Long story," he said. "How about we go back to my apartment and I'll get you something to drink and we can talk there."

She nodded to that and let him help her up. She loved his touch, the solid feel of his hands, and she really loved how he felt against her and how he made her laugh.

And the memory of being in a room like this one was there as well, and the kind people who had helped them all.

But she needed answers.

A lot of them.

A moment later they were in his apartment and he sat her on one side of a large couch. There was a blanket on one side, and as he said, his apartment was full of books and computers as was hers, and what looked to be a couple half-eaten dinners on an end table. Typical bachelor.

It looked like he sometimes slept on the couch facing a wide screen on one wall. She had done her share of falling asleep watching a movie as well and just not bothering to go to bed.

"I have water, fruit juice mix, and water," he said.

"Water," she said.

"Good choice."

He vanished through an archway to the back of the living area. She loved watching him walk and the way he moved. Even after this surprise, which she should have realized wasn't a surprise after this morning's rescue, she was still focused on him.

She needed to clear her mind and ask a lot of questions before this went too much farther.

A few moments later he came back carrying two glasses of water with ice.

He handed one to her and then sat on the couch, turned to face her. She took a sip and the fresh, cold water helped clear her mind a little more.

"So what are Seeders? Aliens?"

"All Seeders are humans," Gage said, smiling. "I'm human in case you were wondering."

"Thank heavens for small miracles. Alien sex would be a little kinky even for me."

He laughed, then set his glass on the small coffee table in front of the couch, pushing away a few books to find room.

"Humans on any planet always believe that they are the only race in the galaxy," Gage said. "And actually, that's true. Most galaxies are empty of any alien life of any type. So the job of the Seeders is to get a planet ready for human life and then seed human and animal life on that planet and then help the human civilization mature through all the problems."

She shook her head not really even understanding what he just said.

"Your home world below was seeded with humans and animal life by Seeders," he said.

"Evolutionary evidence?" she asked, not grasping still what he was saying.

"All planted," he said. "And then Seeders stick around to help each human culture survive all the problem periods and eventually jump into space."

"How many planets have the Seeders done this to?" she asked.

He laughed. "I would have no idea. Maybe all the possible planets in a thousand different galaxies. I don't think anyone knows, honestly, since it has been going on for so long. But the front line of the Seeders finished with the Milky Way Galaxy thirty thousand years ago and has moved on toward all the galaxies around the Andromeda Galaxy. I understand that this galaxy now holds about four hundred thousand human worlds. At least ones that have survived."

She couldn't even begin to imagine that scale.

"So have you ever met an alien?" she asked because she flat couldn't think of anything else to ask.

"There are no aliens that humans in any galaxy interact with. We just leave them alone in their own galaxies and move on."

She nodded. "So only humans?"

"Only humans," he said, smiling at her.

Then she remembered he had said he was four hundred plus years old.

"How do you live so long?" she asked.

He shrugged. "When I was recruited as a Seeder because I have some special gene, I just basically stopped aging and I don't get sick and I learned a bunch of other fun stuff like how to teleport."

"So Seeders are a giant force of babysitters," she said, "over younger or hurt societies."

"Some are," he said, nodding. "Others are on the front lines preparing planets and doing the hard work of getting human cultures started on new planets. And still others are explorers, going ahead of the front lines to explore galaxies to make sure there are no alien cultures."

"So are all humans Seeders?" she asked.

He laughed and shook his head. "Seeders are pretty rare and are only myths in most human societies. Most Seeders have already moved on before a human culture makes the jump between stars and realizes all that's out there are other humans. And the Seeders that stay around and help cultures keep their identity secret, as I have to do when we are down in Portland. From what I understand, even the myth of there being Seeders falls away for most cultures after a few thousands of years."

She just looked into his green eyes, trying to even form another question. Then she remembered this morning.

"So why rescue me?"

"I was assigned to watch you when you left the city and protect you," he said. "My team, that consists of me and three others, are protecting four others who are considered special."

"So I'm special?" she asked, not really sure she liked the sounds of that. "Why?"

"Besides all the reasons I find you amazingly special, funny, attractive, and fantastic in bed," Gage said, "I honestly don't know. They say that you and I

and the other four all have special Seeder genes."

"So I could become a Seeder and live forever and teleport around?"

Gage shrugged. "I have no idea, actually, but if you are game, I would be up for finding out. My team was never told why we were to protect certain people in Portland, but to just do it."

She shook her head. "I'm really glad you were there this morning."

"So am I," he said, reaching forward and touching her arm.

His touch felt wonderful and calmed her some.

She took another drink of water and put her glass down beside his on the coffee table. "Let's get more information. My brain is near explosion, but we might as well light the fuse. Realized I wouldn't be buying any of this if I hadn't remembered being on the ship before."

He laughed and nodded and pulled her to her feet.

He touched his ear. "Gage Teal and Angie Park to speak with Chairman Soma if possible."

He smiled at her and shrugged after a few seconds of silence.

After another moment a man's voice filled the room. "I would be honored. In my office."

Gage squeezed her hand and again they jumped to a new place.

TWELVE

GAGE SMILED at Chairman Soma who still wore sweat pants and a tight body shirt. One thing about running a ship of a few hundred thousand people, you could do what you wanted it seemed if you kept the ship running smoothly and making a profit.

Gage introduced Angie and Soma shook her hand.

"Chairman Soma is in charge of this entire ship," Gage said. "Seeder ships run as businesses, so the Chairman is the head of the ship instead of a Captain as in a military structure."

Angie nodded and said, "I like that."

They remained standing and Soma explained. "I called for Chairman Ray to join us. He is a few galaxies away so will need to make a few jumps to join us."

Gage just blinked and glanced at Angie, who had her mouth slightly open and her eyes blank even trying to imagine that.

So far she had been amazing in the shock of suddenly finding herself in orbit. Far more amazing than he had been the first time it had happened to him.

But the idea that it would only take a minute for Chairman Ray to travel the distance between galaxies was just stunning to him. And he had been around Seeders for four hundred years.

"So how are you feeling about being on this ship?" Soma asked her.

"I was on a ship like this one once before in the rescue operation," she said. "So not as much of a shock as it would have been."

Soma nodded. "We expected as much. Has Gage given you a rough history of the Seeders?"

"He has," she said, smiling at Gage. "But I have a thousand more questions."

"If you wouldn't mind," Chairman Soma said, indicating a desk to one side of his room, "You can learn the history of the Seeders in just a few short seconds while we wait for Chairman Ray."

Angie looked at Gage and he nodded and smiled. "A quick and fast education system. Doesn't hurt."

He had used that system to pick up a lot of extra information on various things, including the entire history of the Event that hit this planet.

She stuck out her tongue at him and moved to the desk.

Chairman Soma just handed her what looked to be normal padded headphones and said, "Put these on."

She did and then on a heads-up virtual display near her he tapped in a code.

She closed her eyes and Gage just watched her. He had a hunch he would never ever get tired of just watching her as he had done over the last months.

After about forty-five seconds she sighed and removed the headphones.

She looked at Chairman Soma and then at Gage. "Amazing, just amazing."

He remembered that was exactly how he felt when he was finished with that quick lesson about the Seeders.

At that moment Chairman Ray appeared, smiling.

His long hair seemed to flow down his back and he was still dressed in a black silk shirt and slacks.

"Angie Park," he said, stepping forward. "it is an honor to meet you."

"The honor is mine," she said, bowing slightly.

There had been a little bit about Chairman Ray in the learning, if Gage remembered correctly.

Soma indicated they should all sit and Angie moved toward the couch and Gage stayed beside her. Soma and Ray sat in the chairs facing the couch over a wooden coffee table.

"I imagine this is very overwhelming," Ray said.

"It is," Angie said, "but it explains a lot about what happened after the Event when I found myself on one of these ships and also what happened today when Gage saved my life. But what I don't understand is why me and why now?"

Gage had those exact same two questions.

"Why you is simple," Ray said, smiling.

Gage was amazed how Ray just radiated control and confidence and calmness.

"You and Gage both have special Seeder genes in your bodies."

"Genes beyond the normal that it takes to be a Seeder?" Gage asked, surprised he had been included in that sentence.

"Very much so," Ray said. "And there are four more in Portland at the moment with the same gene. You six are the only ones in this entire part of this galaxy that we have found so far. And to be honest, there are fewer than six more in this entire galaxy and all of them are not in positions of knowledge and abilities that you six have."

"Not at all sure what that means," Angie said.

Gage looked at her and shrugged. He felt just as confused.

"It means we have a very special mission coming up that we need the six of you to lead," Ray said. "And that explains the 'why now' of your question. We have been preparing ships for this mission for almost a year. We are within six months of having all preparations complete. We only lack the three special teams to chair the three ships."

"Mission to where?" Gage asked.

"A very distant galaxy that has not been explored," Ray said. "I will fill you in on more details once you both have

had time to think about this. But I can tell you this, you will be chairman of a very special ship. The fastest and most modern Seeder ship ever built. And over a million people will go in each ship with you."

"Each of us would have a ship?" Gage asked, feeling very confused.

"No," Ray said. "The two of you will be Chairmen of the same ship together. It is why the special gene is required."

Soma nodded and then said to Ray, "The other two teams are coming on board now."

"Let me guess," Gage said, "Benny Slade and Gina Helm are one team."

Ray nodded.

"And Carrie Noack and Matt Ladel are the other two? Those are the four besides Angie my team has been protecting."

Ray again nodded.

Angie looked surprised. "I know and like all four of them. Did any of them know about this ship being here?"

She glanced at Gage who only shrugged.

Soma nodded. "Benny and Gina knew. But Carrie and Matt will be having a similar reaction to yours."

"But because of the special gene, they will also remember the rescue," Ray said.

"I would suggest," Ray said, standing, "that the two of you get some rest and talk about this. And we will meet with the others and make the same offer. Then the six of you might want to get together tomorrow."

Gage glanced at Angie as they both stood.

Then Gage turned back to Ray. "Just so I am clear, could you summarize this offer one more time?"

"We have built three of the most modern and fastest Seeder ships of all time," Ray said. "We will give the two of you as a team the chairmanship of one of those ships. Your first assignment will be to travel with the other two ships to a very distant galaxy to explore and discover what is there."

"Chairmen?" Gage asked.

"Chairmen," Ray said.

Soma laughed. "Trust me, you will want to take this offer. This is a great job."

All Gage could do was nod. In four hundred years it had never occurred to him that he would ever be the chairman of his own ship.

Not once.

THIRTEEN

ANGIE FELT LIKE everything since she met Gage at the restaurant has been a dream. She half expected to wake up in her bed cuddled with her two cats.

The wonderful dinner full of laughs, the fantastic sex, the promise of honesty which led her back to the spaceship she remembered after the event.

That ship hadn't been a dream, but then the offer to basically be the captain with Gage of a massive ship full of people just made her shake her head. She had a slightly different gene. She doubted that qualified her for such a task.

They promised they would talk with Chairmen Ray and Soma in the morning and he teleported them back to the large empty observation lounge overlooking Earth below. It was beautiful, with half the planet in night and the stars beyond it.

Gage put the two chairs side-by-side and they both sat down and then he took her hand and they sat there, staring out into space, just thinking.

His touch felt right in her hand and she really, really wanted to spend a lot more time with him. But working together on a vast trip together seemed a little much for someone she had only met this morning.

And the knowledge she had been given about the Seeders and their mission and how they did it in general was stunning. And logical. And massive on a scale she couldn't begin to yet imagine.

And what it took to seed a human world was flat amazing.

An advance Seeder ship would basically wipe out any lower level life on a planet deemed to be in the right orbit around the right kind of star in the right area of the galaxy. They would do that by smashing a large asteroid into the planet.

Then they would return in a few hundred years and start seeding plant and some lower level animal life. And over ten thousand years they would eventually seed a population of humans on the planet as well.

Then Seeders would watch over each planet, sometimes calling in full ships to help a civilization get to the next level. She found it interesting that all Seeder cultures became capitalistic and democracies.

Except for the Seeders themselves. They were pure capitalism, with every Seeder on every ship and on every planet drawing a wage. But Seeders themselves had no government. They basically just kept moving, doing the same thing from galaxy to galaxy and when decisions needed to be made, there seemed to be a number of elder Seeders who just made them.

It was the cause that kept Seeders moving and interested. Helping new cultures come to life on millions and millions of planets.

She glanced at Gage who seemed to just be staring off past the planet into the stars, lost in his thoughts.

"Does it worry you that we haven't known each other very long?" she asked.

He glanced at her and smiled, which made her feel instantly better for some reason. "Actually, a little. But remember I've been following you on your missions out of Portland now for six months. I know how smart and brave you are."

"And foolhardy," she said.

He laughed, which seemed to almost fill the empty ballroom with light, it sounded so perfect to her ears. "A little of that as well."

Then he seemed to think of something and shook his head. "Now I get it."

"Get what?" she asked.

He laughed again, this time to something he was thinking about.

Then he turned to her. "I've been wondering why us, the six of us? Besides the surface element that we have the right genes, why us."

"I wondered the same thing," she said. "Clearly the special gene develops in every galaxy."

"Foolhardy is the answer," he said, smiling at her and squeezing her hand.

Then he turned and faced her completely. "There is something that basic teaching program about Seeders doesn't talk about. That is that, when all the planets in a galaxy that survive expand out into space, they form this fantastic community. But from galaxy to galaxy, the human populations of a galaxy eventually just find a balance and stay in that balance."

"They stop expanding and exploring?" she asked, feeling very surprised that humans would ever do that.

"Exactly," he said. "My small galaxy has already reached that point and no one much does anything about thinking of getting to this larger galaxy so close."

"So to do a major risky mission as Chairman Ray made it sound," she said, "he needs young blood."

"And military training," Gage said, pointing a finger to himself. "Since there are no aliens and all humans eventually learn to get along from planet to planet, the Seeders have never needed much of a military force. And on most planets in my small galaxy, any military has been disbanded a thousand years before I was born."

"Now that makes more sense," she said, nodding. It really did. And the idea that Chairman Ray was looking for someone with experience in being brave and exploring made her feel a lot better. She was damn good at that.

He looked at her, smiling and shaking his head.

"What?" she asked after a moment.

"This morning you were trying to help tell people about the rebuilding going on," Gage said. "Now you are thinking of exploring space with an almost total stranger at your side."

She laughed and reached over and kissed him, which felt flat wonderful.

Then she asked, "What did you say about foolhardy?"

"Not your middle name I hope?" he said, smiling at her. "Angie Foolhardy Park just doesn't have a ring to it."

She kissed him again and then said, "I kind of like it, actually."

"After that kiss," he said, "so do I."

FOURTEEN

HE JUMPED THEM both back to her apartment on the surface and after a snack of cold chicken and an attempt to watch a movie in her book-filled living room, she fell asleep.

Once again he sat on her couch with her head on his lap, just staring at her. She was so beautiful with her long black hair and her wonderfully smooth skin, he could just watch her for hours.

At one point he noticed the movie was halfway over and he hadn't taken his gaze from her. But they both needed some sleep. They had major things to talk about tomorrow.

He eased out from under her and then picked her up in his arms, surprised at how light she felt. He wouldn't mind carrying her to bed every night.

She managed to wake up as he put her on the bed enough to mutter that she needed to use the bathroom.

He just sat there waiting for her, studying her bedroom and all the books and knickknacks in it that made it hers. When she came out of the bathroom she was naked. And the sight took his breath away.

It was like someone punched him in the gut.

She crawled into bed, then said, "Get undressed, silly. And turn off the light."

Then she gave him a sleepy smile before closing her eyes and going back to sleep.

She was clearly very comfortable with him being there with her. Just as comfortable as he was being there.

So he got undressed and joined her and the next thing he realized sun was peeking around the blinds on the window and she was laying in bed facing him and petting one of her two cats.

When she noticed he was awake, she said, "Do you think I can take my cats?"

He laughed. "You will be in charge of the entire ship. You can take anything or anyone you want."

"Will your team come along?" she asked.

"I sure hope so," he said. "But it will be up to them. I'm betting they will."

He moved over and cuddled beside her and she moved the cat to a position on top of her hip.

Touching her felt fantastic. Just the feel of her skin sent electric shocks through his body.

"What are you thinking about all this?" he asked after a moment.

"If you weren't here looking handsome beside me," she said, "I would have thought yesterday all a dream just like the first time on that ship."

"Very real," he said.

She touched his arm and said, "Yup, very real."

He stroked her side and shoulder.

"I know it's real," she said after a moment of thinking. "And honestly, I woke up thinking we should take the job."

He looked up into her wonderful dark eyes. "Even if we end up not getting along?"

"I hope that never happens," she said. "But if it does, we'll work it out I'm sure."

"I hope it never happens either," he said, kissing her. "But you know I have never been great at long-term relationships."

"That makes two of us," she said. "So we figure it out together."

She pressed into him and the cat left the bed in a hurry, and the next thirty minutes were amazing.

FIFTEEN

ANGIE COOKED a quick breakfast and she showered and got dressed in fresh clothes. This morning she put on a white blouse with a sports bra under it and jeans and clean tennis shoes. She put on two small pearl earrings as well.

Then he jumped them to his apartment and she sat on the couch in his living room and looked at his books on his coffee table while he showered and got ready as well.

She loved how comfortable she felt in his place. Except for the cats, it felt just like her apartment. And they even had been reading some of the same books.

When he came out of his bedroom and she glanced up, her breath again caught in her chest for a moment. He had to be the most handsome man she had ever seen. He had on jeans, a light T-shirt that didn't hide any muscles, and his short dark hair still looked damp. He smiled when he saw her and the smile reached his wonderful green eyes.

"You are just stunning," he said, coming up to her as she stood.

"I was thinking the exact same thing about you," she said. Then she kissed him long and hard.

"Start that and we'll never get out of this apartment today," he said, laughing as the kiss finally broke.

"And what would be wrong with that?" she asked, smiling at him.

"Absolutely nothing," he said. Then he kissed her back, long and equally as hard.

Finally, breathless, she pushed him away and said, "Can I take that for a promise for later?"

"For any time," he said, smiling at her.

"All right, then," she said, adjusting her clothes. "Let's go find out what this new job is really all about."

He nodded, then touched something in his ear she would have to remember to ask him about and said, "Chairman Soma, do you have a few minutes for Gage Teal and Angie Park?"

A moment later Soma's voice came back clear to Angie. "It would be an honor. In my office."

"Is this honor thing normal?" she asked Gage just before he jumped them there.

"Not in the slightest," he said.

Chairman Soma stood from behind a huge wooden desk and came around to shake both their hands.

Chairman Ray had been sitting on the couch and he stood and also shook their hands, smiling.

"I just finished speaking with the other two couples again this morning," Ray said, "and it seems they are all very interested in hearing more about the job. Have you decided to join us as well?"

Angie was surprised at that, but only slightly. She glanced up at Gage who was looking at her with those wonderful green eyes.

"Well?" she asked.

"I'm game if you are," he said.

"I am if you are," she said.

Then she turned back to Ray. "It seems we also are interested in hearing more."

"Wonderful," Ray said, smiling.

Chairman Soma seemed to be beaming like a proud grandparent watching his grandkids grow up.

"So what is the next step?" Gage asked.

"We need to give you both advanced Seeder training," Ray said. "We will need to do that on my ship. It will take about twenty minutes and another hour to answer your basic questions."

"And this training is different from what I took originally," Gage asked.

"It is," Ray said. "It will activate the special gene both of you have and answer so many questions."

Angie nodded. "At any point, Chairman. Before I get cold feet."

Gage had told her it had taken only a few minutes for him to go through the basic training and learn how to be a Seeder and understand Seeders at a base level. But she really had no idea what she was about to learn or experience, even after the short introduction program last night.

Gage laughed. "Ready as I'll ever be considering I have very little idea what this is really all about."

Ray smiled and then turned to Soma. "We will return here in just over an hour."

Soma nodded and a moment later the three of them were in a conference room with a large wooden table surrounded by leather chairs.

A beautiful woman with short black hair stood facing them. She had on a black silk pants suit and pearls around her neck in a choke-collar fashion. Angie felt she radiated not only incredible beauty, but a depth of knowledge and age, even though she didn't look much over forty.

"This is my wife and co-chairman, Tacita," Ray said.

Gage bowed slightly and said he was honored.

Angie did the same, feeling stunned.

Tacita smiled at both of them. "The honor is mine, I assure you."

"We have one more jump to make to our ship," Ray said.

He moved over beside Tacita and as they touched, the four of them appeared at the top level of a massive room.

Angie had no sense about how far they had jumped, but she had a suspicion it was a great distance. At some point she hoped to really deeply understand the distances and even how large a galaxy really was.

A good dozen people were working around the room at stations on three levels. A huge screen filled one wall and two massive chairs sat in the lower level facing the screen. The two chairs looked like they were molded together.

This was clearly a command center of a massively large ship.

"Wow," Gage said, looking around. "Is this a mother ship?"

"It is," Ray said. He indicated they should come over to the left of the room and sit in two chairs side-by-side.

"Well," Gage said to her as they sat down. "Here we go."

"Together," she said, smiling at him.

He nodded and smiled back. "I like that part."

"So do I," she said as they both placed their hands where Ray told them to.

And around her the massive control room just vanished.

SIXTEEN

GAGE PUSHED BACK from the console when the machine released them.

He felt as if an entire library had been downloaded into his mind and sorted and stored. He knew it was there and knew he could access it all with a thought.

He was amazed he didn't have a headache.

And now he understood far more about what being a Seeder really was. He knew the entire history, everything, about them, and what fantastic work they did making sure humanity got a start in as many galaxies and on as many planets as they could.

It made him very proud of the work he had done in a small way over the last four hundred years.

He knew that, barring an accident, he would now live basically forever. He had sort of realized that before, but never given it much thought and now was not the time either. Living forever and not aging had never been a consideration for him.

He stood and helped Angie to her feet. Her eyes looked sharp, focused.

She turned with him and both of them bowed to Ray and Tacita.

Gage knew that Ray and Tacita were the first chairmen of the very first mother ship and that right now they were thirty or more galaxies away from the Milky Way Galaxy.

Gage turned to Angie. "Are you all right?"

"I am filled with awe and amazement and thankfulness and wondering why I was given this honor," she said, softly.

"We can explain it all," Ray said. "Let's go sit and talk."

A moment later the four of them were back in the comfortable meeting room where they had met Tacita. Different forms of drinks and snacks were aligned along one wall. Gage was surprised he felt hungry, but he did, so he made himself an iced tea and took a large, fresh-feeling glazed doughnut.

Angie got herself a cup of hot tea and three peanut butter cookies.

Then all four of them sat at the end of the large table and just talked.

Angie had the most questions, but she clearly knew the answers almost before she asked them. And he knew the answers the moment she did as well.

They really had been picked because of the special gene they both had been born with. And that gene allowed them many things. It allowed them to remember things and details over centuries of time. It allowed them to teleport vast distances, far more than any regular Seeder. And it allowed them to co-chair a mother ship.

Gage didn't know the mission that they were being recruited for, but he had a hunch it was because of their ability to co-chair the huge ships. Until today he had never been on a mother ship, and actually thought them a myth.

Finally, Ray returned them to Chairman Soma's office with the plan that he and Tacita and the three couples would meet for the first briefing on the coming mission in five hours.

Gage was looking forward to that.

Angie was holding Gage's hand and when they appeared in Soma's office, without Ray, Gage said, "Thank you for the use of your office for all of this."

Soma bowed deeply to them. "It has been my honor. And please, if there is anything I can do to aid you or your mission, do not hesitate."

Gage told control that two were going to the surface and jumped Angie and him back to her apartment.

She first went and found both of her cats and petted them while he sat on the couch. Then she came back and sat down beside him.

"I have to be dreaming," she said.

"The fact that I am with the most beautiful woman on the planet is a dream," he said. "Not sure what you are dreaming about."

She laughed and took his hand and leaned her head against his shoulder.

They sat like that for a few wonderful minutes, both lost in their own thoughts. Then she said, "The Seeders are amazing. How have they managed to just keep going and going for hundreds and hundreds of thousands of years?"

"Fresh recruits like us," he said and she nodded.

"Ray and Tacita want that freshness for whatever they have in mind," Angie said. "That much is clear."

"Very clear," he said. But darned if he could really figure out what the mission might be considering what he now knew about Seeders. This had to be something very new. And that excited him.

"It makes me sad that so many human civilizations just stagnate inside their own galaxy," Angie said.

"I'm not sure if having a galaxy spanning civilization could be called stagnating," Gage said, laughing. "But yes, it does seem that by taking out of most populations the Seeder gene as recruits, eventually the desire to move outward by every culture is replaced by a desire to remain solid and happy and working in other things besides exploring."

"You think the Seeder gene is what always made humans look to explore?"

"As logical as anything," he said.

"So what do we do now?" she asked.

Gage smiled. "We have hours. I am thinking a leisurely walk to one of the fine restaurants in this neighborhood, then back here for some private connection time, then off to the meeting with the others."

She pushed off his shoulder and looked at him, smiling, the smile in her eyes as well. "You think an early dinner might get you into my pants?"

"A guy can hope," Gage said, smiling back.

"Okay," she said. "I suppose I can be bought, but I'm not cheap."

He laughed. "All right, I'll spring for dessert as well."

"Deal," she said, and kissed him.

And they damn near skipped the dinner. They would have if they both hadn't been so hungry.

SECTION TWO
The Mission and Getting Ready

SEVENTEEN

ANGIE FELT EXCITED to see the other four members of this mission. She had known and liked all four of them.

Ray had said the briefing would be in Chairman Soma's office and she and Gage had been the first to arrive.

Soma greeted them with a bow and asked what he could have brought in for them to drink. Both just asked for water.

A moment later a woman's voice in the air said, "Chairman Soma, Gina Helm and Benny Slade asking permission to come to your office."

"Please," he said, and a moment later they both appeared.

Gina was tall and lanky and looked strong, far stronger than Angie. She had dark, short hair and wore a white long-sleeved blouse with the sleeves rolled up and jeans.

Beside her Benny was as tall as Gina, but far wider and very muscled. He was ex-military and it showed in his posture and short, dark hair, cropped close. He had also been originally from New York and had saved many lives there by setting up huge buildings as refuges after the Event.

As a couple, Benny and Gina had always intimidated Angie, but she had really come to like them over the last year since they came to Portland from New York.

Both of them smiled when they saw Angie and they both hugged her, congratulating her on joining the Seeders.

Then Angie introduced Gage.

Benny smiled. "So it's your men who have been keeping an eye on us over the last six months."

"They that obvious?" Gage asked, laughing.

"Not in the slightest," Benny said. "In fact, they are damn fine."

"Good to hear," Gage said. "I'm hoping they'll join up to come along on whatever we are going to be doing."

"That would be damn great if they would," Benny said.

At that moment Chairman Ray appeared with Carrie Noack and Matt Ladel. Both were looking a little shocked and Angie didn't blame them at all. She was feeling the same way.

Carrie was a tiny woman and all muscle. She had short brown hair and very light skin. She wore a blue blouse and jeans and tennis shoes. Matt was as tall as Gage or Benny at six foot, and he too was all muscle. He had short brown hair that Angie had never seen combed and large brown eyes.

Angie went and hugged them both and the others congratulated all three of them for joining the Seeders.

Angie felt so much better now that Carrie and Matt were here and she wasn't the only new blood in the room. And having her there also seemed to bring Carrie and Matt back into their eyes a little as well. Clearly Chairman Ray had been giving them extra help over the last few hours.

Angie felt lucky that she had Gage beside her.

After the bottles of water for everyone arrived, they all sat in Chairman Soma's couches and chairs. Only Ray remained standing and Soma went around behind his desk to watch, but be out of the picture.

At that moment Tacita appeared beside Ray and bowed a greeting to all of them.

Angie just felt in awe seeing her and her amazing beauty.

"It's time we tell you what this is all about," Ray said. "We have been planning this for about three years now, since we found all of you with your special genes during and around the rescue operation here."

Angie was sitting next to Gage in one of the big chairs and she reached over and took his hand. She noticed that Carrie and Matt were also holding hands on the couch and Benny and Gina also held hands across two chairs.

Clearly Ray and Tacita had recruited three couples.

"All of you now know from your training," Ray said, "how very rare true alien advanced life is throughout the known universe."

All of them nodded.

Angie had been surprised at that more than anything else in the vast learning from this afternoon. Most galaxies had no growing or even starting alien sentient population. And Seeder scout ships spent a vast amount of time searching before any Seeder ships entered the galaxy to start seeding.

And on any galaxy that alien life was found, no matter at what level, the Seeders simply watched in secret and the seeding ships went around, leaving the entire galaxy to the alien race.

Very, very few alien races ever made it off their original planets and only two alien races had made it to other stars before falling back into ruin and then destruction. Without Seeder help, almost all human worlds seeded would face the same exact fate. Even with Seeder help, many still did.

It seemed it was very, very difficult to survive as a culture and expand into space.

And that was not counting the natural disasters that almost wiped out the human population on the planet below.

Ray went on with Tacita standing beside him saying nothing.

"Three years ago this was found in deep space heading for an edge of this galaxy," Ray said.

A hologram of what looked like a blackish pile of wadded-up junk appeared floating in the middle of the room. The pile of junk was clearly artificially constructed, but Angie could make no sense out of it at all.

"This is an alien ship," Ray said. "It is the size of a small moon, larger than even Seeder Mother Ships."

Angie was stunned, as she could imagine those that found the alien ship had to have been. Seeder Mother Ships were also the size of small moons, but shaped like a bird in flight, not like a pile of junk.

"The ship has been on trans-tunnel drive for about two hundred thousand years. The shields of the ship failed about a hundred thousand years ago. Nothing is alive on the ship."

Stunned silence filled the room as they all just stared at the hologram of the alien ship floating in the middle of the room.

Angie had a very hard time imagining two hundred thousand years. That number just seemed impossible.

"Are the alien drives designed for flight speeds between galaxies?" Gina asked.

Ray nodded. "They were. Basically just trans-tunnel drives, taking all fuel from the space it traveled through. We have been studying that ship now for the last three years. Every detail of it."

"What did the aliens look like?" Benny asked. "Were you able to tell that?"

Angie wasn't sure she wanted to know that, but was glad Benny asked.

"Short mammals with fur on their bodies," Tacita said. "Two arms with hands with six fingers on each hand. Legs used for climbing as well as grasping. A moderate brain capacity."

"They looked something like this," Ray said, "from what we have gotten out of the records on the ship and from what remains of those on that ship that were protected."

An image of a very alien creature appeared in the air. It looked like a cross between a badger and a raccoon, only with a huge head and huge and powerful shoulders and arms.

"Rats," Benny said. "They look like damn rats. I hated those things in New York."

The alien had close-set dark eyes and a long snout with sharp-looking teeth, so

Angie could see where Benny from New York thought that.

"They stand about two feet tall," Tacita said. "Very powerful."

"Damn large rats," Benny said.

Ray went on. "From what we could tell from remaining records on the ship that we have been able to translate, they could have up to thirty offspring, lived between twenty and thirty of our years, and were extremely aggressive."

"So why the mess of a ship?" Benny asked.

"This is what their original ship looked like," Ray said.

Angie watched as the hologram shifted to a sleek arrow with six fins.

"As something went wrong on their mission to a nearby galaxy," Tacita said, "and they found themselves going into deep space with no hope of finding a nearby galaxy soon, they started to build onto their ship to allow for the extra population growth."

"They managed to scoop up materials from the vacuum of space just as trans-tunnel drive takes power from the slight particles in deep space. They created this ship, along with ways of feeding the constantly growing population."

The hologram slowly morphed into the image of the ball of trash that had been there before. Only now Angie could see the ship inside the additions.

"They made it work for almost a hundred thousand years," Tacita said, "before the ship's systems collapsed from overload and their shields failed."

"At three generations every one hundred years," Gage said, "that's impressive. Three thousand generations were born and died on that ship. Wow."

Angie just stared at it, feeling a deep sadness for alien creatures that had died

a very long time ago just trying to stay alive.

Even if they did look like rats.

EIGHTEEN

GAGE FELT STUNNED by all that he had heard so far. Aliens had actually developed a society that had managed to get out of a galaxy. That was both exciting and scary beyond words.

And to hear about the tragic tale of this one spaceship was amazing.

In the advanced information they had gotten earlier, he now knew what all the aliens Seeders had discovered over the years looked like. Spider-like creatures with large brains, other mammal-like creatures like these, and even some strange squid-like creatures that had actually managed to get to their nearest star systems.

"So what mission are you thinking of us doing that concerns this alien ship?" Gina asked, looking away from the ship to Ray.

Angie and Gage did the same, Angie squeezing his hand.

The hologram of the ship vanished showing a mostly two-dimensional illustration of a vast number of galaxies. The galaxies were no more than points of light and the hologram looked more like a white cloud floating there in the air.

"This is cut along the lines the alien ship traveled in two hundred thousand years of trans-tunnel flight," Ray said.

"Wow, that's a lot of distance," Benny said.

"It is," Ray said. "The small dot here is the Milky Way Galaxy and Andromeda Galaxy and other local group galaxies and all of these other dots are galaxies or clusters of galaxies the ship got near, but clearly not close enough to help them with whatever problem they were having."

Gage watched as a line appeared from the Milky Way back through all the other dots to one galaxy that must have been the start of the two hundred thousand year voyage.

"We believe the ship started here," Ray said.

The dot expanded to become an image of a group of galaxies. The line ended in the center one.

"We think the ship was trying to reach this galaxy," Tacita said, and one of the close galaxies to the main one lit up. "But something went horribly wrong and they passed the galaxy by and went onward."

"We do not know from the records we have translated so far if this was just a standard milk run, or the first exploration run to another galaxy," Ray said.

The hologram vanished.

"What we are hoping you can do with three new ships," Ray said, "is go find out what these aliens are up to and if they are expanding in this direction and so on."

"In essence," Tacita said, "a scouting mission."

Gage sat back and Angie squeezed his hand.

"I'm just a little confused," Matt said. "Are you asking us to go on a two hundred thousand year one way mission?"

Ray shook his head and smiled. "No, thanks to two brilliant inventors who actually met in orbit over this planet during the evacuation ten days after the Event, new breakthroughs have happened in trans-tunnel drive."

"The first breakthrough since humans left our original galaxy," Tacita said, "besides making the drives safer."

"So how long should this trip take?" Gina asked.

"At full speed of the new drives," Ray said, "about ten years. But we expect you will do a little exploring along the way, so a little longer."

Gage again just shook his head. He couldn't even imagine that speed and not even the training earlier today on the real scale of Seeders helped him with that.

"Two hundred thousand years down to ten?" Gina said. "How is that even possible?"

"In short," Ray said, "trans-tunnel drive opens up a tunnel through space so that a ship can travel far, far faster than the speed of light."

All of them nodded. Gage understood that as well. He even knew the math of it from his college days.

"What the two new brilliant inventors did was figure out a way to open multiple tunnels inside open trans-tunnel flights."

"Basically," Tacita said, "If you are going ten times the speed of light inside one tunnel, and then open another tunnel inside that tunnel going ten times the speed of the other tunnel, it factors to a hundred times higher. These inventors have come up with a way to open ten tunnels inside each other safely if needed."

Gage just sat there shaking his head. He and Angie were going to lead one of three ships to visit the first aliens to ever create a culture that could leave its own galaxy.

It was no wonder Ray and Tacita wanted young people who were used to the unexpected and had lived with that being normal. There was no telling what they would run into on the other side of that ten-year journey.

And no telling what they would find along the way, either.

Damn, this was scary.

And exciting.

NINETEEN

ANGIE WAS STARTING to feel overwhelmed again. But with slow breaths, she just let her new learning from earlier kick in.

The woman who had been helping find new people to tell about Portland yesterday was at a slight war with the woman who was now a Seeder and knew all the history and details of being a Seeder.

Yesterday she thought that aliens didn't exist and humans were the only ones in the galaxy. She had been partially right about the humans being the only ones, but now she knew aliens clearly did exist.

Just an unimaginable distance away.

Across from her Carrie and Matt were also looking somewhat shocked. And neither had said much at all.

It was Benny who again broke the silence in the room by asking the next obvious question, but one Angie had not thought of in the slightest.

"What kind of ships will we be using?" Benny asked.

Ray nodded and a hologram of a beautiful spaceship appeared floating in front of them. It had the look of a beautiful bird in full flight. The front was a long neck and the nose came down to what looked to almost a point.

"Three identical ships," Ray said. "Each are mother ships in size and will carry over a million people each."

Angie just opened her mouth, then shut it.

Over a million people?

Her stomach twisted into a knot.

"Each ship will have two hundred scout ships, a couple hundred seeder ships, and two hundred military ships as well," Tacita said. "All equipped and built with the new drive."

"These three new mother ships are state of the art," Ray said, "with full shields and defensive and offensive weapons capabilities, something we have never built into a mother ship before now."

All Angie could do was sit there and stare at the beautiful ship with her mouth open.

"The ship's names?" Gina asked.

"Gina, you and Benny will command the *Star Rain*," Ray said.

Angie liked that name.

"Carrie and Matt, you will command the *Star Fall*.

Angie liked that name as well.

And Angie and Gage, you will be in command of the *Star Mist*."

Angie instantly loved the name.

Matt finally spoke up. "I am not certain why you think that Carrie and I can command a ship carrying more than a million people into a situation as you have described."

Beside him, Carrie nodded and Angie felt herself nodding as well.

Ray and Tacita both smiled.

"The advanced training you all took to be sitting here," Ray said, "is just the tip of the knowledge. Once you have been accepted by your ships, which are sentient in their own ways, you will be given the next stage of training."

"So we will be trained?" Angie asked, feeling very relieved on hearing that."

"Completely," Tacita said. "Just the first basic part will take nine days. And you will always have your ship to help you with anything you need."

Silence for a moment as that sank in.

Then Ray went on. "Over the next six months you will be in charge of picking your crew and getting to know your ship completely. Carrie and Matt, we will help you with the crew aspects of things. But as Chairmen of a Seeder mother ship, your command is your command."

"We believe you all will be perfect for this critical mission," Tacita said. "We need your youth and ability to think in any situation."

Suddenly Angie realized how Ray and Tacita were talking. This was a very, very rare position. And why Soma had bowed to them.

"Without any more hesitation," Tacita said, "we would like to introduce you to your ships. And give you the information you need to make a real decision."

Benny and Gina nodded.

Angie looked at Gage who smiled and nodded.

"Why the hell not?" Angie said.

Ray looked at Carrie and Matt, who seemed to just sort of be staring at each other.

"Would you two like to meet *Star Fall?*" Ray asked.

Matt nodded first. Then Carrie nodded and smiled.

"It is a beautiful name," Carrie said. "So as Angie said, why the hell not?"

Ray turned to Chairman Soma. "Would you show Angie and Gage the command center of *Star Mist* and the command chair?"

Soma stood and bowed slightly. "It would be my honor."

And a moment later Angie found herself standing in a massive command center next to Gage and Chairman Soma.

"Welcome, Chairmen," a soft female voice said not only out loud, but seemingly in Angie's head. "I am *Star Mist.*"

Angie suddenly felt at home.

TWENTY

GAGE WAS ONCE again stunned at the size of a command center on a mother ship. And how comfortable he felt standing in it.

The ceilings were far overhead and the room had three levels, each about two steps higher than the one below it.

The back level was the highest and went halfway around the room, filled with stations on both the walls and facing inward. From the looks of it, a good forty people could work on this level if needed.

The next level down was also a half-circle, with all the stations facing a massive wall screen that had to be two stories tall and even wider.

On the lowest level, right in the center was what looked to be two massive, high-backed chairs that were molded together, facing the screen.

The Chairmen's chair.

His and Angie's chair.

And then *Star Mist* said in a very warm and soothing female voice, "Welcome, Chairmen. "I am *Star Mist.*"

Beside Gage, Chairman Soma bowed.

"It is an honor to meet you," Angie said, also bowing slightly.

"It is my honor as well," Gage said.

"Thank you," *Star Mist* said.

Gage looked at Angie, whose eyes were wide and she was smiling.

"Chairman Ray would like me to show you your command chair," Soma said, indicating they should go down to the lower level. "From there *Star Mist* will give you a sense of your ship."

Angie took Gage by the hand and led him down the two levels. All the stations along the way were dark, but he had a hunch he would know what each station was for very shortly.

When they stepped down onto the lower level, Chairman Soma stopped on the second level.

Clearly being on the command level was only for the two of them.

The command chair was stunning in design. One piece molded plastic with what looked to be comfortable cushions.

"The chair will form to your size and shape," *Star Mist* said.

"Thank you," Angie said.

"You are welcome," *Star Mist* said.

Gage turned to Angie. "Are you ready? Because I have a hunch when we sit down in this chair, everything will change for us."

Angie nodded. "I can't say I'm not scared out of my mind right now."

"More than facing those people in the compound the other day?" Gage asked, smiling at her.

"No, not that kind of scared," she said, laughing. "Scared of the unknown, the future, my ability to do this wonderful task that has been offered to us."

"I feel the same way," Gage said, squeezing her hand. "So let's be scared together."

"Deal," she said.

She smiled and kissed him.

And then holding hands, they sat in the big chair together, she on the left, he on the right.

Instantly the chair started to form around them and Gage felt it shape to fit his body perfectly. And it fit perfectly where he held Angie's hand.

The chair actually came out over the top of them, placing them in a sort of shell with the open side facing the huge screen as they tipped back slightly.

"Wow, this is comfortable," Angie said.

"Perfect," Gage said.

And then suddenly Gage could feel and sense Angie beside him. He couldn't read her thoughts, but he felt closer, like they were a team connected completely.

She turned and smiled at him and he smiled back.

"Like that closeness?" he asked.

"More than I want to admit," Angie said.

And Gage could sense and feel *Star Mist* as well, as if just on the edge of his thoughts.

"May I start by showing you the layout and progress of construction?" *Star Mist* asked.

"Please," Angie said.

Gage could feel her excitement and her worry, both. Somehow, *Star Mist* had linked them lightly together through the chair.

And almost instantly Gage could sense he knew the ship, where the three major ship's hangars were, how many thousands were working on *Star Mist* at this very moment and what they were doing.

It felt as if he was inside *Star Mist*, the personality of the ship, and knew her.

And knew what she knew about the ship.

And he felt he liked her at once.

"Wow," Gage said after a moment. "Very impressive."

"Thank you," *Star Mist* said. "Construction is on schedule."

"Very good to hear," Angie said.

"Now I need to take you to meet with Chairman Ray and Chairman Tacita," *Star Mist* said. "Please do not be alarmed. This will only take a moment."

The shell of the chair closed in over them, leaving them holding hands but slightly in the dark.

Gage could sense Angie's sudden worry, but he had a hunch it matched his own.

There was a slight sense of movement, then the front of the chair opened back up and it was clear to Gage they were no longer on board the ship.

Star Mist said simply, "Welcome to Earth."

Every planet humans settled was called Earth. Gage's home world was called Earth, as was Angie's. But the way *Star Mist* said it, and he was connected to *Star Mist* now in his mind, he knew, without a doubt, he was on the very first Earth.

The actual birthplace of all humanity.

And that just scared him more than he wanted to admit.

TWENTY-ONE

ANGIE HAD A HUNCH she knew what *Star Mist* meant when she said, "Welcome to Earth" from Angie's earlier training. But she didn't want to think about that. And yet she knew because she felt connected to Star Mist at a very deep level.

And that connection felt comfortable and right.

In front of them was a massive circular room with two levels. They and the command chair were on the top level with nothing else around them and what looked like a plain wall that closed in the room around the top level with large pictures of stars and planets giving the wall color over the grayness.

In the center of the room, five steps down were a couple dozen couches and chair arrangements with end tables and coffee tables. A table with snacks and drinks ran along one side. All were in brown shades and a few small flowering plants separated some of the chairs and couches from others.

There looked to be a light brown carpet on the floor.

Surprisingly for the size of the large room, it felt comfortable and she could smell a light odor of baking bread.

"You may leave the chair," *Star Mist* said. "I will wait for your return."

"Thank you," Gage said before Angie could.

"You are more than welcome," *Star Mist* said.

Gage helped Angie up and they stepped out of the chair and down the five steps from the top level.

Angie still felt slightly connected to *Star Mist*, even when not sitting in the chair. That felt comforting, actually.

Then Gage pointed. "See all the rings?"

Angie could see that all the way around the top level were rings in the floor spaced evenly. The *Star Mist* command chair sat in one of the rings, the molded, high-backed chair standing proudly, but all alone at the moment.

"A meeting place for all Seeder mother ship chairmen," Angie said, softly. "Wow."

She just felt stunned. And considering how many trillions of human planets in thousands and thousands of galaxies, only having this many slots for mother ship chairmen was frightening. There couldn't be more than a hundred around the room, if that many.

After learning about the Seeders yesterday, she had wondered how the Seeders made decisions and it seemed she had just gotten her answer.

And now it looked like she and Gage were part of that very limited group.

They were in way, way over their heads.

Of that she had no doubt.

As they were about to turn toward the couches, another chair shimmered into place beside their chair and then opened up, all without a sound.

Benny and Gina sat inside, holding hands, their eyes wide.

"Welcome to Earth," Angie heard *Star Rain* say to them.

"The *first* Earth?" Gina asked.

"It will all be explained," *Star Rain* said. "I will wait here for your return."

Benny and Gina stood from the chair and saw Angie and Gage standing there. They came slowly down the five steps, looking around as they did.

"Looks like they are set up for a party," Benny said.

Then Benny looked at the top level and saw all the rings and then the two command chairs filling two of the rings.

Angie could tell he instantly understood.

Benny and Gina stood, looking around at all the rings, then Gina said, "Wow, are we in the fricking deep end of the pool."

"I feel like a kid with a pedal bike with training wheels being asked to ride a Harley," Benny said.

All three of them laughed at that. Angie was feeling the same way. All this was happening so fast.

"You all right?" Gina asked Angie.

Angie just smiled. "I am so far past my comfort zone, I can't remember what

it felt like. So thanks to Gage here, I'm just going forward."

Gage laughed and said, "If you think all this is just a daily happening for me, we need to talk."

She laughed and squeezed his hand. "Who knows what lurks in a guy's past."

"Not this," Gage said, waving his arm at the large room, "I can assure you."

At that moment another chair shimmered into place beside the other two and opened up to show Carrie and Matt sitting, holding hands, eyes wide as well.

They both looked to be on the verge of complete panic.

"The children are all here," Benny said. "Now where the hell are Mom and Dad?"

TWENTY-TWO

THE SIX OF them finally moved down to the couches and food. All of them took a bottle of water and a few cookies, just talking about how out of place they all felt.

And way over their heads.

Having all of them feeling the same way seemed to help Matt and Carrie and Angie a little, but Gage couldn't even imagine what they were feeling right now. His transition into a Seeder had been fast, but over a six-month period where he had managed to get used to spaceships and flashing around in space and helping human cultures and so on.

These three were only on their second day and in a position where someone was telling them they were going to be responsible for a million people. He didn't feel even close to ready for that. And he was over four hundred years old.

He was the oldest of them all by far, actually, since Gina had been a Seeder for just over a hundred years and Benny for less than four years. So he couldn't imagine how they were all feeling if he felt completely overwhelmed.

Finally, after about ten minutes, another chair shimmered into place almost on the opposite side of the large room and it opened to show Ray and Tacita.

They were holding hands and Ray helped her up from the chair and the two of them walked hand-in-hand to the group. The two of them still clearly loved and respected and cared for each other.

And the rumors were that they were hundreds of thousands of years old.

Gage sure hoped that he and Angie could be still feeling that way in ten years, let alone in thousands of years. Considering both of their problems with relationships in the past, that was going to be a question.

Right now he would just take tomorrow with her, he felt that lucky.

Tacita had them all sit on couches together, one couple per couch. Then she and Ray took chairs facing them.

"So is this really the original Earth?" Gina asked.

"It is," Tacita said, nodding. "You will learn the complete history of mankind over the next few days as you go through the training."

"Nothing whitewashed or left out," Ray said. "It was a bumpy path to where we find ourselves now."

"No other way with humans," Benny said.

"So true," Ray said, smiling.

"How many Seeder mother ships are there?" Gage asked.

"At the moment, counting your three, twenty-seven. But others are built and in transit empty to various galaxies, and others are in construction as well."

"We need many more, "Tacita said. "That's why bringing three more mother ships into active duty is such a special event.

Gage was surprised there were so few. Very surprised.

"And we were picked to be the chairmen of the three new ships because of our special genes?" Angie asked.

"Yes," Ray said, "partially. But you were mostly picked for your youth. You will understand far more after your training."

"So what exactly is to happen next?" Benny asked.

Gage had been about to ask that same question.

"You have nine days in a row of extensive training here," Tacita said. "We will return after each session to eat with you and answer questions anyone has. Between sessions you can go back to your homes and rest and talk."

"This first session will not only give you a history of all of humanity," Ray said, "but trigger your advanced genes to allow you to be in better contact with your ships."

"All three of your ships are very pleased with each of you," Tacita said. "They will become your friend, your constant companion, and be there for anything you need."

Gage squeezed Angie's hand and she smiled at him. In the background he could still feel *Star Mist* with him. And he liked that feeling.

"They will help us get past this feeling of being totally inadequate?" Matt asked.

"They will help, yes," Ray said, smiling. "And the teaching coming up will help as well. We would not put you in charge of a Seeder mother ship for such an important mission if we did not believe you could handle the task. And the ships would have also rejected you if they felt that you were not up for the job."

Matt nodded.

Gage also nodded.

Ray and Tacita stood.

"Now take your partner's hand," Ray said, even though all three couples were holding hands already.

"And relax," Tacita said.

As Ray and Tacita turned to move away, an opaque bubble formed around each couple and then snapped down tight over them.

Gage could feel a massive amount of information flowing to him.

He could also feel Angie beside him and through her hand.

And together they went down into the flow of knowledge.

TWENTY-THREE

THE NEXT NINE days seemed to go by instantly to Angie, yet they took forever at the same time.

The first session had lasted three hours and she felt like her head might explode with the vast amount of information. But at the same time, she felt calmer and also she could sense *Star Mist* was with her.

And she could also sense Gage. It felt like she was no longer alone and she loved that feeling.

After every learning session each day, Ray and Tacita joined the six of them for dinner in the large room to answer questions.

As each day went by, Angie felt more in control, more sure that she and Gage could do what they have been asked to do.

And it was clear that the other two teams felt the same way.

By the time the teaching was over, and they were having their last dinner together in the main room, questions had turned to the coming mission and the final construction of the three ships. And how to pick and recruit the crew for not only each mother ship, but for all of the smaller ships on board.

After each day during the learning period, Angie and Gage had gone back to her apartment in Portland. They had taken a nap in each other's arms, then walked down to the first restaurant they had eaten at and had a quiet dinner, not really talking about anything, but just being together and letting the information soak in.

Then each night they had gone back to her apartment and made love. And with each day, she had felt more and more connected and in love with Gage at such a deep level, she couldn't believe that level had even existed.

So on the afternoon before the last day of learning, they had decided to jump to the chairmen's living quarters on *Star Mist*.

The huge apartment had taken Angie's breath away. It wasn't furnished, but it had four bedrooms. Two for beds and two for offices. It had a huge living room with a stone fireplace. There was a kitchen and dining area that was a dream, with every modern appliance she could imagine and a few she didn't know the function of as well.

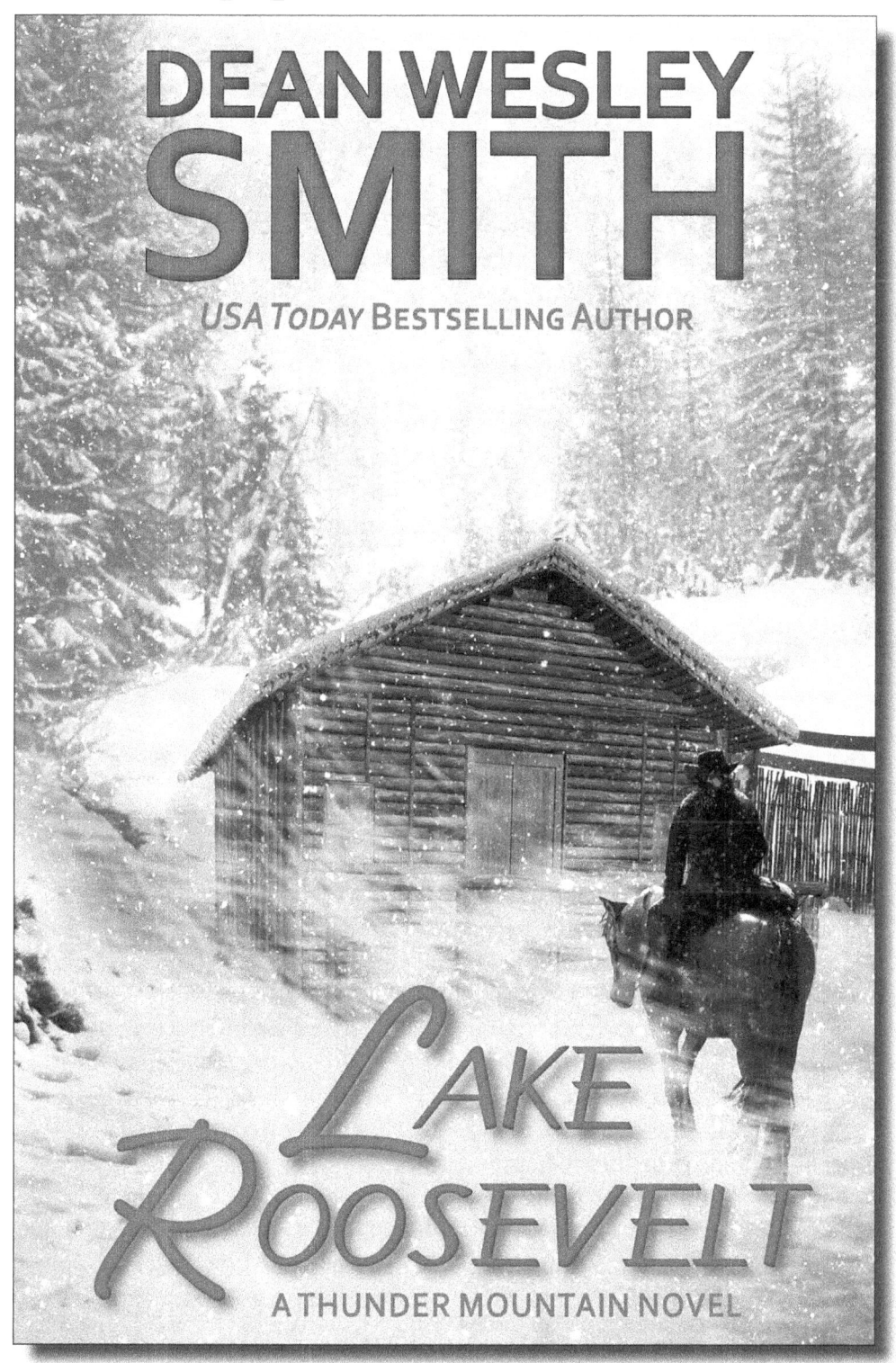

She had felt instantly at home, even though there wasn't a stick of furniture in it.

Instantly.

They had wandered through the huge place, hand-in-hand, including standing in the two monster walk-in closets that were larger than her bedroom back in Portland.

And the apartment had a bathroom off of each walk-in closet and another major bathroom near the fantastic living room.

"We've known each other for just under two weeks," Gage had said as they stopped on the edge of the living room and he took her in his arms. "You ready to move in with me?"

"Pretty fast there, lieutenant," she had said, smiling up and him and then kissing him.

Then she had eased back and looked at the man she had completely fallen in love with and that she felt she now knew better than any person she had ever met.

"On one condition," she had said.

He smiled and had said, "Name it."

"That we only have one huge bed in this place, so we can always sleep together."

He had laughed. "Deal."

Now, as all eight of them sat having a wonderful dinner turkey and dressings and some side dishes after the last learning session, the mood was excited and even Carrie and Matt were feeling completely confident.

Angie loved the food. After the learning sessions, she always felt so hungry. And she flat couldn't believe her mind had been able to grasp everything that had gone into it. Yet it had.

"I have one question that seems to be nagging in the background," Benny said.

"Fire away," Ray said.

"There seems to be a fear of this alien race," Benny asked. "Is that because human cultures become so passive over time?"

"Exactly why," Tacita said. "There are entire galaxy-spanning human civilizations that have existed for hundreds of thousands of years that have no military ships or even would think that way. Most human cultures would have no way to resist an aggressive alien culture if attacked. Too many centuries of breeding that nature out."

"Again why the youthful leadership of this mission," Matt said. "Makes sense."

Angie nodded to that. It made complete sense now.

"So why do Seeders have no historical memory?" Gina asked. "Why are entire galaxies just left on their own to have the fact that they were seeded fall into myth and legend?"

"Human nature," Ray said, shrugging. "When there is no threat, humans don't care about where they came from, what is on the other side of the same galaxy, or even on the other side of their own planet."

That was so true Angie didn't want to think about it.

"We tried to maintain a cultural memory for the first few hundred galaxies we helped start with human life," Tacita said. "But it never held and no one seemed to care and we eventually dropped the idea."

"Do all the chairmen meet at one point or another?" Gage asked.

Angie realized that wasn't in the information they had been fed either.

"They do," Ray said. "Every year. We meet here and have dinner and talk about the future and how everyone's projects are progressing. Next meeting is in about two hundred days. We will let you all know ahead of time, I promise."

"We do it on the anniversary of the launch of the first mother ship to seed another galaxy," Tacita said.

"When was that?" Angie asked, again wondering why that information wasn't in the rest of what they had learned.

"About six million years ago," Ray said.

"Wow," Angie said and the others seemed just as impressed.

Seeders had been moving from galaxy to galaxy for over six million years. How had she become so lucky as to get to be a part of all this?

"Whose ship was that?" Benny asked, taking a second helping of the fantastic smelling turkey.

"It was our ship," Ray said, smiling at Tacita.

Tacita nodded. "We took it out and I can remember the fear like it was yesterday."

Ray gently rubbed Tacita's shoulder with affection before both of them went back to eating.

Angie and everyone else at the table just stared at Ray and Tacita.

And it took a moment before anyone else took a bite of anything.

TWENTY-FOUR

OVER THE NEXT six months after training, it surprised Gage of how much needed to be done. And the five who lived in Portland had to come up with reasons for leaving the city for an extended period of time so that no one would notice that they had vanished.

Angie had moved her two cats into their apartment on *Star Mist* and the two

cats took to it without a problem, clearly enjoying the extra room to run and not seeming to miss the lack of windows.

Angie and Gage had spent one day furnishing the apartment and stocking the kitchen with dishes and everything else they would need.

Gage loved living with Angie every day as well, and it felt at times they could almost read each other's minds. Not quite, but they clearly knew what each other was thinking most of the time.

And every time they sat in their command chairs, that feeling grew stronger.

They spent a vast amount of time for the first two months overseeing the last of the construction and learning every detail of the moon-sized ship. They knew it from their training, but both of them wanted to see everything firsthand as well, from the storerooms to the hanger decks.

And *Star Mist* helped them make sure they didn't miss a detail.

Gage really loved being so close to *Star Mist* as well.

And Angie had learned quickly how to teleport, which had been a fun day of practice and excitement.

For the next four months, they also worked on putting together a bridge crew. Actually they needed three shifts of a bridge crew, the main shift and second shift and third shift.

Both Angie and Gage agreed that Gage's second-in-command, Drake, should be on the bridge in the main bridge crew and in charge of the entire military side of things for the ship.

Ray and Tacita agreed, so when Angie and Gage explained the mission and offered Drake the job, with the original team helping him in various positions, Drake just damn near lost it.

After he pulled himself together, he had said simply, "Hell yes."

But their best find was their second-in-command of the entire ship, which they put into place five months before launch. They had asked Ray if Chairman Soma would be insulted at the offer and Ray had just laughed. "I doubt it, but you would have to ask him."

So they had talked to Soma and offered him the second-in-command position if *Star Mist* approved him and Soma had said yes instantly.

And *Star Mist* had loved him.

So with Soma working with them and all of his knowledge of what was needed in a bridge crew, the first main bridge crew formed within two months.

And then each bridge crew member suggested others on down below them, and a second shift and third shift bridge crew took shape.

By the time the entire bridge crew was staffed, there was still two months until launch, so they had lots of time to run drills and make sure everything on board was ready. And both Angie and Gage liked everyone on all three shifts on the bridge.

Even though many of the crew members were far older than even Gage, they showed Angie and Gage immense respect. Often more than both wanted.

Gage very much appreciated that.

All three ships' crews came together at about the same pace.

And what Gage found amazing was that the bridge crews of each ship were from fifteen to twenty different galaxies in this area. And many had had hundreds of years at positions with other bridge crews. But it seemed, to be on a bridge crew of a Seeder mother ship that was to

be sent on a very special mission was a real honor.

Not one person turned down the offer.

Almost from the first week after the learning sessions, the six chairmen had made it a habit to meet once a week for dinner in one of the chairman's apartments to talk and plan.

And laugh.

They did a lot of laughing.

Often Ray or Tacita or both would join those dinners.

Those dinners had helped them all get closer. And by the time the week before launch, they knew each other and trusted each other completely.

Gage could not have imagined a better group to take such a risky mission with.

All of them knew the path they would be taking to the target galaxy and had studied it, but what they did along the way had been a matter of discussion.

That was finally settled out during the last dinner before launch.

Gage and Benny as military men had put the plan together and presented it to everyone including Ray and Tacita after a yummy meal of fresh fish and salad prepared by Angie and Matt.

They were in Angie and Gage's apartment, sitting around the large wooden dining table. It was mostly square and Ray and Tacita sat at the end of the table with their backs to the wall, Angie and Gage sat with their backs to the kitchen, Benny and Gina with their backs to the living room, and Carrie and Matt with their backs to the bedrooms.

"Here's Gage and my suggestion for a plan," Benny said. "All three mother ships would head out at near top speed past the range that Seeder scout ships have already explored."

Gage was stunned at how far they were going to go outside of Seeder areas. The distance already explored was less than one percent of the total distance they planned to travel.

"Then in all galaxies near the intended path after that," Benny said, "all three mother ships will stand off the outer edge of the galaxy and launch one-hundred-and-fifty of the two-hundred scout ships to do fast scans of the galaxy looking for alien life and also looking for any signs of the aliens that we are headed toward."

"A military ship will go with each scout ship," Gage said, "for protection and also to help with the scans."

"So the three mother ships would pause near a galaxy," Ray said, "then launch nine hundred ships total to cover the galaxy, leaving one hundred ships in reserve in each mother ship. Correct?"

"Exactly," Benny said.

Gage nodded and went on. "Since all the scout ships and military ships are equipped with the new trans-tunnel drive, the surveys of an entire Milky Way-sized galaxy should take around a week from what we have figured out after talking to experienced survey ship chairmen."

"They wouldn't do as deep a survey as scout ships normally do that takes decades to complete," Benny said, "but they would make sure no aliens existed at any level in the galaxy."

"And if there are aliens?" Angie asked.

"If we find an alien race at a lower level," Gage said, smiling at her, "we go ahead and still survey the entire galaxy and then move on. If we find a more advanced race, then we stand off and take data, but not do a full survey."

"Very good thinking on that," Tacita said, nodding.

"As we have discussed," Benny said, "every bit of data would be returned to the home base now being constructed on the edge of the Milky Way galaxy to track and monitor the mission."

"But by doing it this way, taking our time to get to the target, we get a lot of data collected along the route of the alien ship."

"How many galaxies are you talking about doing a fast survey of?" Ray asked.

"Seven hundred and ninety galaxies of various sizes before reaching the target galaxy," Benny said, "so the trip to target should take around sixteen years, counting the time in transit between galaxies."

Gage was very happy to see everyone around the table nodding at the idea.

"Would all the ships reload back on board the mother ships after each stop?" Gina asked.

Gage glanced at Benny.

"If the distance between galaxies is close, no," Benny said. "But on the longer distances, yes."

Gage took a deep breath and went with the next idea he and Benny had. Neither liked it much, but they could see no choice.

"We also want to send ten scout ships and ten military ships from each mother ship ahead to the next galaxy," Gage said.

"Even with the arms and shield on these three wonderful mother ships," Benny said, "we don't want to drop into the middle of an advanced and armed civilization."

Silence filled the dining area. Gage flat hated this idea, but no military person wanted to go into a possible combat area without knowing what they were walking into. So he completely agreed with Benny.

Finally Ray nodded. "That makes sense."

"A suggestion," Tacita said.

Everyone turned to look at her.

"The scout ships hold upwards of thirty thousand lives, including crew families. Correct?"

Everyone nodded.

"And the military ships we have built hold around twenty thousand crew and family," Tacita said.

"That's right," Benny said.

Ray nodded, clearly understanding where Tacita was going.

"What would be the bare minimum crew that each ship could function with completely?"

Again silence.

"I honestly never asked that question," Benny said.

Gage hadn't either, but he liked where this was going.

"So are you suggesting," Carrie asked, "that the ten scout and ten military ships from each ship set up residences for their crew's families on board the mother ships?"

"Not permanent homes," Tacita said. "Rotate a different ten scout and military ships each time to scout ahead, so each family would only be displaced for a few days every six months or so."

Gage glanced at Benny who was smiling.

"We both hated this idea," Gage said, "because of the great risk of life. This will hold the risk to reasonable levels and we are not asking spouses and children to be in harm's way."

"All know the risks of this mission," Ray said.

"But managing the risks this way for many is a good plan," Gina said.

"I agree," Angie said. "And I like the overall plan of taking our time getting to the target."

"Agreed," Ray said.

"Agreed," Tacita said.

"Then we have a plan," Benny said, smiling.

Gage was smiling as well.

It was time to get moving. And that had him excited, more than he wanted to admit, considering they might be flying into a mess.

A mess that might cost the over a million people on each mother ship their lives.

SECTION THREE
The Journey

TWENTY-FIVE
(Thirteen Years Later)

THE CALL CAME in from the scout ships working ahead on the 614th galaxy that they had found a problem.

Angie had been working on dinner and Gage was in the command center, making sure everything was in good order with the most recent galaxy survey before he came back to their apartment for the evening.

They tended to work all the time, often in their own offices, checking every detail of everything on board the ship. During the day they had made it a habit to get out to either the military area or the scout area to talk with people.

Those on board liked the fact that the chairmen had made themselves open to talk with. It didn't reduce the respect, but actually increased it.

The thirteen years since launch had gone smoothly in all the surveys so far. Out of the six hundred plus galaxies they had surveyed, two had sentient alien life at planetary levels. One was a race of large ant-like creatures with massive heads. The second one was a form of ape-like creatures, very different from humans, but clearly working to build a civilization.

The three mother ships had quickly surveyed the galaxy and moved on.

"Angie, to Command," Gage said, his voice almost echoing through their apartment. In thirteen years, that had never happened.

She wiped off her hands, took off her apron, and jumped to his side in the command center.

"We have a problem up ahead," he said, taking her hand as they sat down in their command chair.

The familiar feel of the chair wrapped them and the heads-up display appeared.

"We are here," Gage said.

"We are linked in as well," Benny said.

"Standing by," Carrie said.

Angie was stunned. They had all practiced linking the ships a few times, but nothing had come up that needed it until now.

"Go ahead, Chairman LeAnne," Gage said.

Chairman LeAnne's face filled the screen for a moment and *Star Mist* fed Angie the fact that she was the chairman of *Blue Bay*, the lead scout ship exploring the next galaxy ahead.

Chairman LeAnne was thin, with very short brown hair and a deep frown on her face.

"We have found a dead galaxy," LeAnne said. "We have only been here and taking preliminary readings from the edge, but something really nasty tore an advanced civilization that had thrived here apart."

"You're going to need to explain more, Chairman," Benny said.

"From our initial scans the moment we dropped out of trans-tunnel drive," Chairman LeAnne said, "we thought we were facing an advanced, galaxy-spanning civilization. All signs were in place. So we all remained completely shielded and made sure no scans could be traced. All our ships spread out around the outer edge of the galaxy to get a clear picture of what was happening."

Angie knew that was all standard procedure.

"Here are some of the scenes we found," Chairman LeAnne said.

An image of a former large city smashed to nothing. Blackness and ruins. There wasn't even any plant life.

Another quick series of images appeared, all about the same showing total destruction.

"All of these images were taken on planets scattered around the galaxy," Chairman LeAnne said.

"What kind of power could do this?" Carrie asked softly, not really as a question, but saying out loud what all of them were thinking.

Looking at the ruins, Angie knew the signs of what she was seeing from what had happened back home.

"This didn't happen that long ago," Angie said.

"You are right," Benny said.

"About fifty standard years ago," Chairman LeAnne said, "from our initial scans. And pretty much to all planets at about the same general time."

"Any idea what this race looked like?" Matt asked.

Chairman LeAnne nodded and then said softly, "They were from our target race."

Angie felt her stomach cramp down into a knot that she had a hunch wouldn't clear for some time to come.

TWENTY-SIX

FOR THE NEXT three hours, Gage and Angie studied all the information coming in, not leaving their command chair. And staying in touch with the other two ships as well.

They called back all ships from their current galaxy and all ships were back on board the mother ships within two hours. Then all three mother ships headed toward the dead galaxy at full trans-tunnel speed.

The scouts, working from the edge of the dead galaxy, discovered what had happened on each planet. Some sort of weapon had basically ignited the entire atmosphere, sending a massive wave of fire and intense winds over every foot of the surface, burning it all and knocking everything into piles of rubble.

Even if one of the aliens had survived that, they died instantly because all oxygen was completely burnt away from the atmosphere.

The scouts also discovered that there were over six-hundred-thousand planets destroyed, all with cities on them. No planet without a colony or a city on it was touched, which eliminated the chance this was some sort of natural disaster.

And every ship in space and every space station was destroyed in the same way.

Every member of the entire alien race had been wiped clean from this galaxy.

Stunning carnage, just stunning. Gage couldn't even begin to wrap his mind around it.

Just about the time Gage was feeling exhausted and famished, Chairman LeAnne asked to be linked to all of them once again.

The three mother ships were still three hours away from the dead galaxy.

When the link to all three mother ships was up, Chairman LeAnne put up a hologram of the galaxy. It was a standard spiral galaxy about half the size of the Milky Way.

"The destruction started here," Chairman LeAnne said, having a red color appear on one edge of the galaxy.

As Gage and everyone watched, the red spread through the galaxy.

"How long did that take?" Gina asked.

"Six weeks approximately," Chairman LeAnne said.

Gage knew exactly why it took that long. It had taken him twelve weeks to get from one side of the Milky Way Galaxy to Angie's home planet in standard trans-tunnel flight. This galaxy was about half the distance across.

"That's the speed it would take at standard trans-tunnel flight," Gage said to everyone else.

"Damn, good spot," Benny said. "*Star Rain*, could you tell us how many ships would it take to do that, stopping at each planet along the way for less than one hour standard?"

"Four hundred and twelve ships," *Star Rain* said.

"I concur," *Star Mist* said to just Angie and Gage.

"*Star Mist,*" Gage said, "assuming the killing fleet left the galaxy approximately at where they finished their attack, what would be their possible next galaxy targets? Please show us all."

"And how long would each possible target take for them to reach at standard trans-tunnel speed?" Angie asked.

"I have illustrated the answer with a sphere to show the farthest distance standard trans-tunnel flight would allow a ship to go from the edge of the destroyed galaxy," *Star Mist* said.

A shimmering three-dimensional image appeared in front of Gage and Angie.

Gage's stomach twisted when he saw there were galaxies inside the sphere.

"How many galaxies are inside that range?" Benny asked.

"Seventeen," *Star Mist* said to all the chairmen.

"Thank you," Angie said, her voice soft.

Gage could tell she felt as worried and upset as he did. Something very, very ugly was happening ahead of them.

"Thank you, Chairman LeAnne," Benny said. "Please continue your research. We will have more help for you shortly."

She nodded and vanished from the link.

"I suggest we all rest and link back up in two hours before we reach our destination," Carrie said.

"I agree," Gina said.

"Two hours," Gage said.

Gage stood and helped Angie out of the chair. The next instant he had teleported both of them to their apartment.

They needed the time to think.

This kind of situation was the very reason Ray and Tacita had picked them.

Now it was time to find out if Ray and Tacita had made the right decision.

TWENTY-SEVEN

ANGIE FELT MUCH better after a light dinner and time to just sit quietly with Gage and think while sipping on after-dinner coffee in front of their fireplace.

She couldn't believe that they were an hour away from a galaxy where just six months before an entire civilization had been wiped out.

She couldn't grasp that amount of death and she sure couldn't grasp any reason for it.

She turned to face Gage. His strong, handsome face looked a little rested and not as haunted as he had looked earlier. And he seemed ready to get back to work.

"The way I see it," she said, "we have some sort of major war going on."

He nodded. "Either between two factions of the same race or two different alien races."

"So what are we going to do either way?" she asked.

"We keep researching what happened exactly while at the same time we find out where the fleet of ships is located," Gage said.

She nodded to that. That was what she had been thinking as well. "But then what? Do we stop the destruction by siding with one side or the other?"

He shook his head. "We cross that bridge when we come to it. But humans have never taken a non-interference stand since the mess in our first galaxy. I don't see this being any different."

"Except we don't interfere with any alien cultures," Angie said. "These are alien cultures."

"We have walked into a mess," Gage said, laughing and shaking his head. "Let's see what the other chairmen are thinking."

Angie and Gage put their coffee cups back on the kitchen counter and jumped to the command center. The main bridge crew was still at their stations and second crew was backing them all up, sometimes with two people working at the same station together. Giving each other breaks and double-checking everything was a standard procedure in these kinds of emergencies.

But this was the first time Angie had seen it in operation outside of a drill.

They dropped into their chair and *Star Mist* caught them up to speed quickly on the reports that had come in.

The other four chairmen had just connected in as well when Chairman LeAnne again signaled she had an update. At this point the three big ships were just over an hour away.

"We found the remains of an attacking ship," Chairman LeAnne said.

"Details and on screen," Benny said.

In front of Angie appeared an image of a sleek, swept-back winged ship that seemed to shimmer against the blackness of space. The ship looked like it could easily go through atmosphere. And it had a fairly close resemblance to a Seeder ship.

The sight of it took Angie's breath away.

"How large is that ship?" Gage asked.

"The size of a normal scout ship with room for about seventy thousand to live," Chairman LeAnne said.

"Survivors?" Carrie asked.

"We are too far away to tell," Chairman LeAnne said.

"Thank you, Chairman," Benny said. "We will be in touch within the next hour, but keep us apprised of any more developments."

Chairman LeAnne nodded and the link broke.

"So who has any ideas?" Matt asked.

Between the six of them they went over what Angie and Gage had discussed.

All of them agreed with sending scout ships after the fleet. But now that they had found a ship that had been a part of the fleet, they all agreed that a few more hours would make little difference. They would first investigate that ship and what it was capable of doing.

They agreed a normal-sized group of scout and military ships would continue on forward to the next galaxy in their plans to see what was there.

And that a group of thirty scout ships and thirty armed warships would spread out in groups of ten pairs going after the fleet to see where it was.

That left most of the scout ships and military ships to go over this dead galaxy with a fine scan, to make sure nothing was missed.

Then it was Gina who asked the question that Angie hadn't thought of.

"Do we bring Ray and Tacita in on all this, beyond sending back all the information we have gathered?"

"Can they get here?" Angie asked. She knew that relay stations were being built out from the Milky Way along their route, and she knew that Ray and Tacita could teleport across vast distances.

"They can get here," *Star Mist* said to everyone.

"How fast?" Angie asked.

"Within an hour," *Star Mist* said.

"I say they need to be here," Benny said.

"I agree," Gina said.

Carrie and Matt both agreed and so did Gage.

"*Star Mist,*" Angie said, "Would you please invite Chairmen Ray and Tacita to an emergency meeting in one hour in our chairmen conference room? Please have drinks and light snacks available for everyone. Inform us all when they have arrived."

"I will do so," *Star Mist* said.

"Thank you," Angie said.

And then for the next hour the six of them went over every detail they knew so far and the three mother ships took up positions in various places around the edge of the dead galaxy.

The next wave of scout ships was sent onward toward the next galaxy and five scout ships surrounded by ten military ships jumped to the location of the invading fleet damaged ship.

Reports would be flowing in soon and they would have a lot more knowledge.

"Chairman Ray and Chairman Tacita have arrived in the conference room," *Star Mist* said.

Angie nodded and somehow felt slightly relieved as she and Gage stood and jumped to them.

TWENTY-EIGHT

GAGE NODDED to both Ray and Tacita as he and Angie appeared and then took their seats near the head of the table. It was their ship, that was their positions.

Ray wore his normal silk shirt and dark pants that seemed to make his long silver hair shine. Tacita wore a dark silk pants suit that seemed to glisten as she walked.

Gage hadn't seen them since launch thirteen years before, but they hadn't changed in the slightest, which didn't surprise him considering their vast age.

Ray and Tacita took seats at the end of the table and a moment later Carrie and Matt appeared and sat down on the left side with a nod to Ray and Tacita. And then Benny and Gina did the same, sitting on the right.

"I am assuming," Angie said, starting off the meeting, "that you have not heard of our discovery yet?"

"We have not," Ray said.

"*Star Mist*," Gage said, "please bring up a hologram of one of the destroyed planets."

City rubble as far as the eye could see and then the hologram pulled back to show the destruction was on a massive scale.

Gage watched as both Ray and Tacita looked shocked.

"Our scouting teams found this on every formerly inhabited planet in this galaxy," Benny said. "Basically the oxygen in the atmosphere was ignited causing a massive fire storm that swept around the globe and destroyed the world."

"The aliens who lived there were the aliens we came in search of," Matt said.

That snapped the heads around of both Ray and Tacita to stare at Matt.

"Bring up an image of the galaxy, please, *Star Mist*," Gage said. Gage knew that Ray and Tacita were not going to like this at all.

The ruins vanished to show the small spiral galaxy floating in the middle of the table.

"Please run how the destruction pattern went through every planet with these aliens on it," Gage said.

The red spread from one side of the galaxy to the other.

"Every planet with a civilization on it in the entire galaxy was destroyed in six weeks, the time it took a ship to travel through the galaxy at standard trans-tunnel speed," Benny said.

Ray and Tacita looked completely shocked.

Gage remembered a few hours before that he felt the same way. In fact, after watching that again, he felt shocked once more.

"It would take a fleet of at least four-hundred-and-twelve attacking ships to do this," Gina said.

"And this all happened six months ago," Angie said.

Gage didn't know what Ray and Tacita were thinking, but their faces had gone cold and hard and actually angry.

"*Star Mist*," Gage said, "please bring up the illustration of how far the attacking fleet could have flown since this attack."

The image of the sphere appeared in the air over the conference table.

"We plan to send out three teams of ten scout ships and ten military ships," Benny said, "to find the fleet. And we have our standard ten scout ships and ten military ships already on the way ahead to our next scheduled galaxy to see what they will find there."

Ray nodded.

"But we have not sent the scout ships after the fleet yet because we found remains of an attacking ship," Matt said.

"*Star Mist*, please show us the image of the attacking ship."

The sleek, shining, winged craft appeared, glowing against the darkness of space.

Ray gasped and Tacita said, "Not possible."

And at that, all six other chairmen turned to look at them.

And if Gage didn't know the two humans sitting across from him were millions of years old, he would have sworn both of them were going to be sick like children.

TWENTY-NINE

"WOULD YOU MIND filling us in on what you are thinking?" Angie asked, staring at the pale faces of Ray and Tacita. They both looked like they had gone into instant shock.

Ray nodded. "You have scout ships moving toward that ship?"

"Scout and military ships are at the ship now," Benny said.

Ray looked at Angie and Gage. "May I have permission to ask *Star Mist* a few questions?"

"Certainly," Angie said and beside her Gage nodded.

"*Star Mist,* would you illustrate with a dot the original galaxy of humanity and the galaxies around it, all on the same scale? Mark the original galaxy by having it blinking."

"Be glad to, Chairman," *Star Mist* said.

A hologram appeared above the table far enough in the air that everyone could still see each other under it without a problem.

The hologram looked to be a vast field of thousands and thousands of stars and clusters of stars, but Angie knew each point was a galaxy with billions of stars. The scale that Seeders worked and thought at still surprised her, even with

the training and the last years of being on board this wonderful ship.

"Would you pinpoint this galaxy on the star field you are showing?" Ray asked.

The scale got smaller slightly and more thousands of points were added until one point of light blinked. It looked like a vast white cloud was hanging over the conference table.

"*Star Mist,* would you show the positions of all of these galaxies three point five million years ago," Ray asked, "adjusting for galactic drift and then draw a line between the two blinking points?"

The dots of light shifted slightly and a line appeared.

"Please now make the Milky Way Galaxy on this chart blink and draw a line from the original galaxy to it as well."

Another line appeared, only shorter. But Angie could see that the two lines formed what looked like a slice of pie out of all the galaxies. And they had just traveled along the crust of the pie to get here.

"*Star Mist,* at standard trans-tunnel drive," Ray asked, "how long would it take for a ship to travel from the original galaxy to this galaxy?"

"One-point-four million years," *Star Mist* said. "Without stopping."

"Oh, shit," Tacita said and put her head down on the table.

Ray just sat back and stared at the image of galaxies floating over the table.

Angie and the rest of the new chairmen just sat silently.

A few moments later, Tacita sat up straight and took a deep breath. Then she said, "I have no doubt that you will find that attacking ship to be of human origin."

Angie kind of had a hunch that was where all of this was heading, but it still surprised her.

"Why would humans wipe out an entire galaxy full of sentient creatures?"

Tacita opened her mouth to say something, but Ray touched her arm and she just shook her head and closed her mouth.

"We're out here risking our necks," Benny said. "And the lives of millions of others. I think we deserve to know what you were about to say."

"They believe they can kill these creatures because they created them," Ray said.

Tacita nodded. "I was not going to put it that nicely."

Angie just sort of stared at both of them. "They create an entire race of intelligent creatures and then destroy them. Why?"

"Why in the early days of all human civilizations do humans use animals to experiment on and then put them down?" Ray asked, anger clearly not far below the surface.

"But this was a galaxy-wide civilization," Carrie said.

"Just a different scale of experiment," Tacita said, almost spitting her words.

Angie felt sick to her stomach. She didn't want to believe that civilized humans were capable of such things. This went against everything the Seeders knew and believed.

"This is disgusting," Benny said.

"They think we are just as disgusting," Ray said.

Angie finally couldn't take it any longer. "Are we going to get to know what happened all those millions of years ago and how you know all this?"

"And why we didn't learn it with the basic briefings?" Gage said.

"We didn't include it because we didn't think it was possible," Tacita said.

"And it happened almost a half million years after the origin of the original galaxy," Ray said, "after we were already Seeding and expanding outward though many galaxies."

"What was possible?" Carrie asked a moment before Angie could.

"We never thought it possible that a fleet of ships could survive over a million year trip through space," Ray said.

Angie looked at the shining ship on the screen, floating dead in space. Clearly they had survived just fine.

THIRTY

GAGE WAS FEELING more annoyed than anything else.

He and Angie and over a million people on this ship had all come out here to risk their lives trying to find out about another galaxy-spanning race and suddenly they learn about some fight between human factions millions of years ago.

Not happy was the least of how he was feeling right now.

And Gage could tell that Benny and Gina and the others were also slowly building to anger.

Gage had a hunch you did not want to see the six of them really mad at anything.

The room was deathly silent and the star field hung high over the table like a bad cloud.

"I would say," Benny said, "that you owe us a story and a real explanation of what the hell is going on."

"Agreed," Matt said.

Gage just nodded, almost afraid to say anything.

Ray and Tacita both nodded.

Gage was sure they could feel the anger building as well. None of the six of them were covering it very well.

And beside Gage, he could feel Angie almost vibrating.

"I can assure you," Ray said, "that it did not dawn on us in any fashion that this alien race might be human created until just now. And we may still be wrong about that conclusion."

"We are not," Tacita said.

Benny held up his hand and stopped them both. "The beginning. Start at the damn beginning, would you?"

Ray nodded, took a deep breath and started into the story. "About a half million years after we first launched our ship to start Seeding other galaxies, we found a new alien race."

"The ants?" Gina asked.

Gage remembered that from their training.

"The ants," Ray said, nodding.

"We chose at that point to develop the policy," Tacita said, "of leaving alien races alone completely, letting them develop or not develop at their own pace."

"But that policy was very, very controversial," Ray said, "because without intervention and help from Seeders, no human-seeded planet would survive through the many steps that destroy a civilization. We learned that with hard lessons."

Gage nodded to that. He knew from the training that the fact that humans survived at all was by sheer luck through numbers of major periods and setbacks along the way. Most alien civilizations the Seeders had found had not.

"So intervention is a way of life for Seeders and we are proud of the work we do," Tacita said.

"But many thought that the same policy should extend to alien races," Ray said. "Many did not."

"Also," Tacita said, "a very strong faction had always been against the terraforming of planets we did as the first step of Seeding. The faction argued that by smashing an asteroid into a planet to clear it off before Seeding new plants and animals, we were possibly destroying an alien life form that might evolve into an intelligent species in a million years or more."

"By simply settling on a planet, they also argued," Ray said, "even without the terraforming, human settlements and civilization on a planet would stunt and destroy any alien life chance at evolving."

Gage could see both points.

"But the data of observations of billions of planets inside the life zone of yellow stars showed that was not going to be the case," Tacita said.

"In fact," Ray said, "before even the first attempt at terraforming happened, the studies had covered just under nine billion earth-like planets in many galaxies, many of the planets very, very old in their life cycles. No higher level life had evolved or emerged."

"We find evolved life now on about one planet in sixty galaxies," Tacita said. "Do the math on that. And none of the alien civilizations we have found evolved to a civilization that could span outside their own galaxy. And only two spread into their own galaxy at all before destroying themselves."

"So there was a division in ideas," Benny said.

Gage was glad Benny was trying to keep this on track.

"A very strong one," Ray said, nodding. "The other side believed in two things we Seeders do not believe in. They believed in helping an alien race evolve when found and they also believed even more in the genetic building of an alien race from life forms found on a planet."

"Seriously?" Gina asked.

"Holy shit," Benny said.

Ray nodded and went on. "They experimented in a galaxy far too close to the home galaxy. They built a race that eventually tried to take them over."

"The fight was short and very quick," Tacita said.

Ray nodded again. "Seeder military ships came in and saved the remains of the human population in the galaxy from the race they had created."

"Let me guess," Benny said, "you destroyed the experiment."

"We did," Ray said, nodding. "We had no choice, for our own safety. The race they had created was a very aggressive conquering-type race that did not believe in letting any other race live, including those who created them."

"Seeders outlawed any form of that kind of experimenting into the future," Tacita said. "It's why Seeders have a firm policy of going around any galaxy with alien life and standing off and just watching and not interfering."

"And why we are out here now," Carrie said, "to learn and watch and make sure this race is not a threat to our Seeded galaxies."

"Exactly," Ray said.

"So what happened next was that even though mostly destroyed, those who believed in helping alien races evolve were still vocal," Tacita said.

"So we helped them build a massive mother ship called *New Life* with hundreds of smaller ships on board," Ray said.

Gage was shocked. "You helped them?"

Ray nodded, his eyes down.

"The agreement was that the crew, just under a half-million people who wanted to take the journey, went into stasis for one million years," Tacita said. "And after that they agreed they would continue on to get as far away from human galaxies as they could as they searched for alien races to help."

"And to build their own?" Carrie asked softly.

"I'm afraid so," Tacita said.

"*Star Mist,*" Ray said, "Using the same star field floating above us, would you please show from the historical records the direction the *New Life* took when it left the original galaxy."

Gage watched as on the star field hologram a red line appeared. It was not on the track of the line directly from this galaxy back to the original human galaxy. In fact, it went off almost thirty degrees to one side and ten degrees higher.

"Could you show the end of the line where the crew would have come out of stasis after one million years?" Tacita asked.

The line shortened slightly.

"Draw a line from that point to this galaxy please, *Star Mist,*" Ray said.

A blue line appeared.

"How long at full standard trans-tunnel drive would it have taken *New Life* to make that journey?"

"One million, two-hundred-thousand years," *Star Mist* said.

Gage did the quick math for himself. One million years in stasis, one-point-two in travel meant there was well over a million years missing. Damn.

"So they have been exploring along that route for just over a million years," Ray said.

Now Available
from all your favorite booksellers
in trade paper and electronic editions.

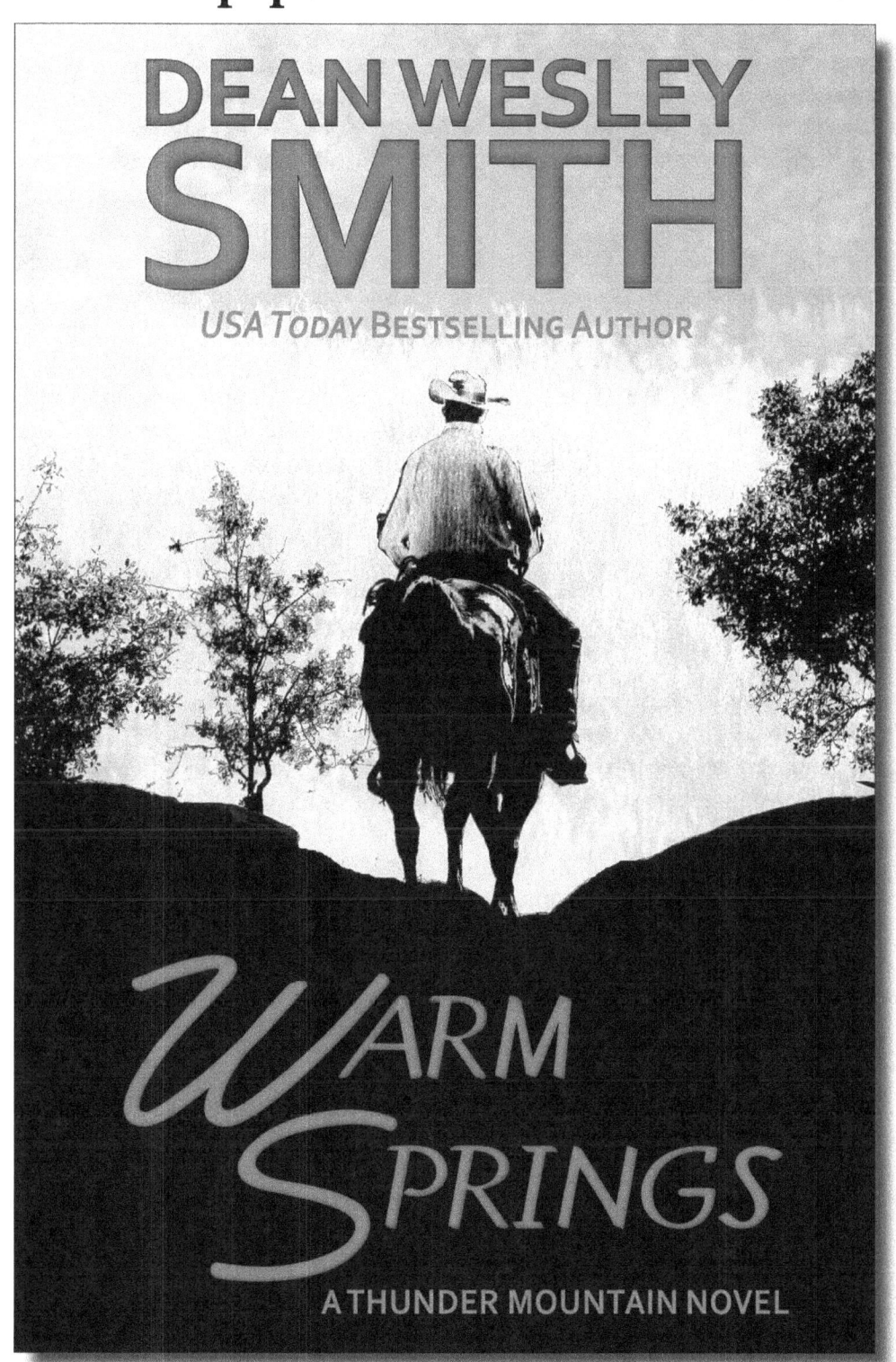

Gage could finally see why this had caught Ray and Tacita by surprise.

"That makes sense now," Benny said, nodding.

He was clearly not as angry as he had been and Gage could feel his anger draining away.

Much better, because now they all had to face the question of what to do next.

SECTION FOUR
The Growing Problem

THIRTY-ONE

ANGIE HAD BEEN so angry that through all of Ray and Tacita's explanation, she had been afraid to say anything or ask a question. She couldn't trust herself to be civil.

But when the original path of the *New Life* was shown, it cleared up to her why Ray and Tacita would not have even thought to mention that part of Seeder history.

Neither of them thought it would apply to this situation.

But now what?

The eight in the conference room were sitting, all thinking, when Angie got a signal from Soma, their second in command. He knew they were not to be disturbed unless urgent, so she clicked it and said, "Yes, Soma. All the chairmen can hear you."

"The scout ships have reached the next galaxy in our original path," Soma said. "The galaxy has been destroyed as well in the same fashion, about six months ahead of this one."

"No signs of life at all?" Angie asked, her stomach twisting.

"None," Soma said.

"Hold a moment," Angie said.

Angie glanced at Gage and then around at the other four chairmen. "I suggest we send the scout ships farther ahead along our intended course."

All five of the other chairmen nodded. Angie did not give Ray and Tacita a vote.

"Soma," Angie said, "please tell the scout and military ships to move on to the next galaxy at top speed."

"I will do so," Soma said.

He clicked off and Angie looked at the others around the conference table. "Seems our distant cousins," she said, "are not only wiping out a civilization that fills an entire galaxy, but one that fills many galaxies."

"We need a lot more information as to what is happening here," Gina said.

"Angie agreed. "For example, how long did it take this race to cover this entire galaxy?"

Gage leaned forward. "Has any information been withheld from us about the ship that started all this and what we learned about this race from that ship?"

"I do not think so," Tacita said, shaking her head.

"They are a race that breeds quickly, is very aggressive, and has little if any arts or music or writing," Ray said.

"Their function was to breed and expand," Tacita said, "which was why they kept adding onto their ship until it finally could not handle any more and failed them."

"They knew that would be the outcome, but they could not stop breeding and adding on new shelter on the ship," Ray said.

Angie shook her head at that. That was deep breeding. They might have survived if they could have controlled that.

"And you saw no evidence of human tampering at all in their records?" Carrie asked.

"Nothing," Tacita said.

"Nothing," Ray said. "But now that we are facing this, we will have the scientists go back and look at everything again with that in mind."

Silence, hard, nasty and uncomfortable silence.

Finally it was Benny who got to the heart of what they were all thinking.

"So do we interfere and stop them or do we stand off and watch?" Benny asked.

Once again there was silence that just seemed to cut at Angie.

"We do not have enough information to act in either direction," Gina said.

Angie nodded to that, as did Gage.

"So we send our scouts and military as planned to find the fleet," Benny said. "Shielded so they cannot be seen."

The other five chairmen nodded.

Again none of them looked at Ray and Tacita.

"And we drag every bit of information and history out of their wrecked ship," Matt said.

Again all of them nodded.

"And we find out if they really did create this alien race and how fast they spread," Gage said.

Again, the other five chairmen nodded.

Angie then turned to look directly at Ray and Tacita. "It would be our honor to have you stay aboard and observe and help us with historical questions. If you would?"

Both Ray and Tacita nodded.

"If you would allow us," Ray said, "we would be glad to put together a historical lesson of the time we described. It would only take a few minutes for each of you to be up to speed on everything about this branch of humanity."

Everyone nodded.

"Thank you," Gage said. "That would be very helpful."

Benny stood. "Let's go find some answers."

With that, he and Gina vanished.

A moment later with a nod to Ray and Tacita, Carrie and Matt also vanished.

Ray looked at Angie and Gage. "We are sorry this possibility did not get discussed and shared."

"We understand," Gage said.

"Yes, we do," Angie said. "But realize you put the six of us in charge of the well-being of millions of people on these ships. We take that responsibility very seriously. That is why we were all so angry at not being completely informed as to what we might be going into."

"We understand," Tacita said.

"Good," Gage said. "So please, in prepping this new historical data, don't leave off any part of humanity that splintered off, or any major lost ships, or anything that might be what is going on here, if that really is a human fleet."

"Let all of us be the judge of what might be important or not," Angie said. "It might be the difference between saving millions or not."

Ray and Tacita nodded and with that Angie and Gage jumped back to their command center.

And for Angie, it felt good to be away from Ray and Tacita. She was still that angry.

THIRTY-TWO

GAGE AND ANGIE spent two hours going over every bit of information coming in, then took a break for a quick bite of lunch, then right back to the command center.

Gage couldn't remember a time before where he had been so focused on one task.

It was at just under three hours after the meeting with Ray and Tacita that the first information started to flow in about the fleet ship.

It was a human ship.

Gage shook his head. Well, that settled that much, but was there another part of humanity that might be out here instead of the ones Ray and Tacita thought were here? That was still to be determined.

The human ship hadn't been attacked, but had engine failure and all occupants had been saved to other ships. The ship was left clearly to be salvaged later.

All systems were still up and running, but no crew were left on board.

The ship had no real weapons compared to the military ships on board *Star Mist*. And the ship only had standard trans-tunnel drives that looked very outdated.

The six chairmen were linked by their ships and had a discussion on what to do next.

"We need the data and historical information from that ship's computer," Carrie said.

Gage agreed as did everyone.

"But we can't leave a trace that we were there just in case we decide to stay out of this mess," Gina said.

"Damn straight," Benny said.

Gage agreed with that, so while they were still linked, they talked to Chairman LeAnne about the possibility of downloading that ship's basic computer on board the ship and not leaving a trace.

"Easily," she said. "We can set up a perimeter to give us warning if one of their ships are headed back and we can have all that data from that main computer system in less than an hour."

"Keep it isolated from your main computers," Angie said. "Extreme isolation. No telling what traps are on there."

"Understood," Chairman LeAnne said and clicked off.

At that moment Chairman Ray contacted them all. "We may have come up with yet another possibility for that fleet being human. And we have the historical data ready to let you all have it quickly."

"We take in the history first," Gage said. "Then we will better understand this new possibility."

Everyone agreed and for the next fifteen minutes, all six chairmen, sitting in their command chairs, absorbed a detailed history of the Seeders after the first millions of years in the original galaxy.

Gage was surprised about the fifty million years after the original galaxy was settled and calmed and the first mother ship was launched. Human history had clearly not gone smoothly.

And there were many small sects of humans who had taken off into space, and one full ship of prisoners that had been exiled in the last days of the final settling of the original galaxy.

Gage was fairly convinced these humans here were not from the exiled prisoners because that ship had been sent in almost the opposite direction. The distance between where it ended up and this location would be impossible to cover even in four million years at standard trans-tunnel drive speeds.

New trans-tunnel speeds could cover it in a few hundred years, but so far there were no signs that this human group had the new trans-tunnel drive.

So which of the many fleeing sects of humanity could this one be?

After they were all finished with the history lesson, it was Matt who suggested they postpone the meeting with Ray and Tacita until they had the preliminary information from the ship.

Everyone agree and Ray and Tacita also agreed, saying that would give them even more time to dig into the types of engines and Seeder ship styles each sect originally left with.

Then, before they signed off, Angie asked the question she and Gage had talked about for only a few minutes.

"Chairmen Ray and Tacita," Angie said, "Could any of the settled galaxies along the way, say two million years ago, moved on into drive speeds that would allow them to leave their galaxy?"

"They almost uniformly do not," Tacita said.

"Almost uniformly?" Benny asked.

Silence.

Then Ray said, "We will do what we can to find out that information as well."

The conference ended.

A few minutes later, as Angie and Gage were going over what they had just learned, Soma reported to them that the

scout ships headed to the next galaxy on their original route had found another completely destroyed galaxy.

Gage just couldn't believe the amount of life, alien or human, that had been lost.

"How much farther to our target galaxy from that galaxy," Angie asked *Star Mist*.

"There are forty more galaxies along the original route," *Star Mist* said.

Gage took a deep breath and squeezed Angie's hand. Then he asked, "*Star Mist*, please link us to the other chairmen again and show us an image of the galaxies surrounding our target galaxy. With the outside edge of the sphere being the galaxy we are now."

The other four came on as the image appeared in front of all of them.

It looked like a ball of bright lights.

"How many galaxies is that?" Benny asked.

"One hundred and seventy thousand," *Star Mist* said.

All Gage could do was stare at that and wonder if this alien culture had spread over all of them, part of them, or even farther.

And how they would even learn that information.

Nobody said a word.

THIRTY-THREE

ANGIE HAD AGREED that they should just send the small group of ten scout ships and ten military ships onward toward their target galaxy, reporting in as they got to each galaxy close along the intended path.

They needed to know how widespread this was.

More information kept pouring in from the damaged fleet ship. It had no shields that could make it invisible as all Seeders ships had standard. It was an old ship as well and had very little fire-power in weapons.

There had been a stockpile of large bombs used to ignite an atmosphere, but the bombs had been taken with the survivors.

When Angie had asked how old the ship was, the answer was not certain, but maybe fifty thousand years, if not more.

Growing up on a young planet where it seemed inventions and jumps forward in science were every day, Angie found it difficult to imagine how little humanity changed over very, very long stretches of time. At some point, when this was over, she would have to ask historians about that.

And why.

Star Mist broke into her thoughts. "The fleet responsible for the destruction has been found."

A moment later all six of them were again linked as the information came in. The location of the fleet, not very far from this galaxy, actually, was shown on a holo-image.

Data scrolled under the hologram. Seven hundred and six ships, with two large mother ships smaller than *Star Mist*, but yet still large. Large enough to carry a half-million people and even more ships.

Large enough to have a factory on board to build more ships as they went.

Angie did not much like that thought at all.

All were clearly human ships and all the smaller ships were designed in the exact same style as the ship left behind.

They were all moving at standard trans-tunnel speeds and were within three weeks of a new galaxy.

All six of the chairmen agreed instantly to have a couple scout ships with military escorts jump ahead to see what was ahead of the fleet.

Suddenly Angie had a worry. "*Star Mist*, from the data so far, did the aliens of this galaxy have a way to warn a neighboring galaxy what was happening?"

"No way of knowing for certain," *Star Mist* said.

"So a ship at full trans-tunnel speed," Benny said, "would only be a few weeks ahead of the fleet. Not much of a warning to mount a defense against what this fleet does."

A few minutes later the scout ships sent ahead reported a full galaxy of teeming alien life, the same aliens that had been in the ship found near the Milky Way.

"We have three weeks," Gina said softly.

No one else said a word.

All Angie could do was stare at the images of planets teeming with life the scout ships were sending back.

An entire galaxy of life.

Seeders prided themselves in building civilizations and saving lives. Could the three-plus million Seeders on this mission just stand off and watch an entire galaxy be wiped out.

Did they even have a choice?

What the hell were the six chairmen going to do?

THIRTY-FOUR

TWO HOURS LATER, the six chairmen were back in the conference room with Ray and Tacita.

Gage hated that they were put in this spot, with an impossible decision. They were going to have to stop a fleet of human ships to save a galaxy of aliens.

But either way, it was now clear they were going to have to jump into the middle of something they did not want to be a part of.

Over the last two hours, the scout ships moving ahead had found another destroyed galaxy. And the data from the fleet's ship left behind had given them the last four hundred and ten years of their trip but not much more in who they were overall.

It seemed that in those four hundred plus years, they had wiped out over nine hundred galaxies full of the aliens.

And they had mapped out where there were even more galaxies full of these aliens that would take them another two hundred years.

It seemed that what had been learned from the derelict ship about the aliens was very true. They were low-level intelligence, had somehow managed to get and be able to replicate trans-tunnel ships, and they could spread over an entire galaxy of planets, adapting to local conditions in under six hundred years.

That was stunningly fast.

With the help of *Star Mist*, Ray and Tacita had a short presentation about the history of the aliens.

"They started here," Ray said. He had *Star Mist* pinpoint a galaxy on a hologram that floated above the table in a red dot. "They spread like this in just under a half million years."

Gage watched as a red tide swarmed out of the one galaxy, mostly moving in one direction.

"We have no information as to the chance they also spread in other directions," Ray said.

"*Star Mist,*" Gage said, "please pinpoint the galaxy we are at now."

A white light blinked on one of the galaxies near the edge of expansion.

"The ratio on that is that every one galaxy they settled spawned at least three more," Ray said.

"A form of exponential growth," Matt said, softly.

"Shit," Benny said.

Angie just sucked in her breath and Gage couldn't believe what he was seeing.

"They must move on," Tacita said, "because they not only are constantly having over thirty offspring in a very short lifetime, but they use up each planet's resources very, very quickly by constructing buildings and millions of ships."

"Most die left behind on planets that are overcrowded and without resources," Ray said. "Basically, every planet the aliens settle becomes exactly like the ship we found."

"Overused and dead," Tacita said.

"This galaxy the fleet wiped out was in the final stages of life," Ray said. "It had been drained of all resources by the aliens, all ships that could be built had been built and were on to other galaxies, and the hundreds of billions of aliens on these planets had already turned on each other for food."

Silence.

"They were eating each other?" Benny asked.

Ray nodded.

Intense silence in the conference room.

Gage couldn't think of a damn thing to say after that.

THIRTY-FIVE

ANGIE SAT WITH everyone in silence for a moment. She always said that Seeders worked at a grand scale, but basically putting down an entire galaxy, like putting down a sick dog, was not at all what she was thinking.

She looked at the hologram floating above the table. The red was like a giant stain of blood covering it.

Then she had a horrid thought.

"*Star Mist,*" Angie said, breaking the silence. "Could you run a simulation of the expansion of this alien race, left unchecked over the next million years? And please mark on the scale humanities home galaxy and the Milky Way Galaxy."

The hologram shifted to what looked like a fine cloud of dots in the air over the table with the Milky Way blinking and humanity's home galaxy blinking.

"I will run this in one hundred thousand year increments," *Star Mist* said.

The red started as a small stain in one area of the dust field. It stopped and Star Mist said simply, "First Segment."

The next image had the red creeping out into a far larger red stain among the white points of light that indicated entire galaxies.

The third had the stain taking up a large area.

It was at the sixth expansion that the red stain covered the Milky Way and the seventh expansion covered the historical home for all of humanity.

"That's enough, *Star Mist*," Angie said. "Thank you."

She felt sick and once again there was silence in the room.

This time it was Benny who broke the silence. *"Star Mist,* would you bring the scale back down to the current area of the alien infestation and then overlay what we know of which galaxies the fleet has destroyed?"

The hologram again changed. The alien galaxies were represented in red, the fleet-destroyed galaxies were represented in green.

Angie saw the pattern at once. The fleet was trying to cut off the leading edge, leaving the galaxies in the center to just collapse on themselves. The fleet was trying to slow down the expansion.

And they were losing.

They were losing big time, actually.

"Shit, just shit," Benny said.

Not a person in the room could disagree with that statement.

Finally, as Angie sat staring at the images where the aliens were expanding, Gage said, "We still need a lot more information here."

"Agreed," Gina said and Angie nodded.

"Do you know who those humans are in that fleet?"

"We think we do," Tacita said, nodding. "And we were slightly wrong about our previous assumption. This fleet is not the humans who broke from the Seeders because they wanted to create alien creatures."

"Then who are they?" Benny asked.

"They call themselves The Exterminators," Ray said. *"Star Mist,* please show the timeline I gave you for The Exterminators."

The hologram of the galaxies faded and a timeline came up floating in the air.

"The fight between the Seeders," Ray said, "which Tacita and I led, and those who wanted to help alien races, and even

create them, ended just about a half million years after we left our galaxy with the first mother ship."

"Because they had created a nasty race we had to destroy, all laws changed against them. We allowed those who called themselves The Creators to take the ship out a million years as we told you," Tacita said.

"But that decision was not a popular one either," Ray said.

"To say the least," Tacita said. "A man by the name of Chairman Wanderson put together a fleet that would follow the first ship and clean up after them and their mistakes. He felt it was the only way to save humanity and over a million people signed up to go with him. They called themselves The Exterminators."

"That fleet is The Exterminators," Ray said. "Or part of them or what is left of them after all this time."

Angie tried to grasp what she had just heard. "Are you saying that maybe this alien race that will sweep over our known universe was built by a group called The Creators?"

"We don't know for sure," Tacita said.

Ray shook his head. "Considering this alien race does not have the mental ability to invent trans-tunnel flight, let alone slow their own reproduction so they don't eat each other, it seems likely. This race should have destroyed itself on its home planet in the normal evolution of their species."

"So this other group is trying to clean up the mess from the first group?" Benny said.

"Seems very, very likely," Ray said.

"I would say it's about damn time we talk to both groups," Benny said.

Angie wasn't so certain about that.

And honestly, she had no real desire to talk with a group that could create an alien race as an experiment or one who could wipe out galaxies full of an alien race.

THIRTY-SIX

THE MEETING BROKE as all eight chairmen went to get more information. Angie and Gage had spent the next two hours in their command chair and not a one of the two shifts of the command crew had left other than to take a short break or get some food.

Thirty scout ships and thirty military ships surrounded and shadowed the fleet, carefully trying to tap into any data they could without raising alarms or letting anyone know they were there.

Every bit of information had been captured from the fleet's ship and from that it was learned that Ray and Tacita were right. This was one of The Exterminator ships. And The Creators were not far beyond the galaxy the mission had been aiming at originally.

At one point the two groups had joined forces to stop the expansion, even though for centuries before, they had had running pitched battles. But it seemed that by the time some sanity had taken hold in the two groups, it was too late.

Now both groups were just fighting a losing battle as the race one group had created swallowed one galaxy after another faster than they could be stopped.

The Creators had given their creation the ability to build an exact pattern ship with trans-tunnel drive. Basically a transport ship. The desire to build the ship and expand into space had ended up being part of the alien driving needs, just like eating and creating offspring.

And the aliens built the ships by the millions on any planet they reached, using all resources of the planet, then jamming the ships full and sending the ships off into space to find new planets or galaxies.

It was why the aliens on the ship they found nearing the Milky Way had been unable to fix their ship. They were smart enough, barely, to build with a pattern, not smart enough to fix the ship when it broke down.

Gage couldn't get the image of this rat-like race overwhelming the Milky Way galaxy like a tidal wave swelling up over a flat beach. Humans would be defenseless at such an onslaught of sheer mass of numbers.

It seemed very clear to him now that this mission was going to be a humanity rescue mission and a mission of death to swarming masses of rat-like aliens.

He flat didn't see a choice.

They all decided they needed some rest before they made the next decision.

He and Angie had gone back to their apartment. They had both worked to fix a small, light meal, then they took a shower together and crawled into bed.

Gage woke about three hours later and Angie was already wide awake beside him.

"What are you thinking about?" he asked, moving to put his arm over her to hold her while she stared at the ceiling.

Even under this kind of extreme stress and on very little sleep, she was still the most beautiful woman he could ever imagine.

"We have to show every member of the crew of every ship," she said, "everything we know, including the outcome of these aliens being left unchecked."

He hadn't thought about that at all, but he agreed.

"We have been carrying a few hundred Seeding ships and crews," she said. "If we decide to help with stopping this alien culture from expanding, we need to let everyone who has problems with that decision head back home on a Seeding ship."

He understood exactly what she was saying. No one should be forced to help destroy galaxies full of aliens.

"I agree," he said. "But we might find another way."

"I love you for your optimism," she said, turning to kiss him.

After a moment of holding each other, something that gave him strength, he said, "Ready to go back to work?"

"No," she said. "But it seems a million or more people and the fate of all humanity says we should."

He laughed and watched her as she rolled out of bed and headed for the bathroom.

It was going to be a damn long day. He knew that, but together, they would get through it.

Somehow.

THIRTY-SEVEN

GAGE AND ANGIE spent two hours letting *Star Mist* catch them up on all the new data coming in about the fleet, about the original creators of this race, and about the fight to stop the expansion.

As they had clearly realized yesterday, the Exterminators and the fleet of Creator ships were fighting a losing battle. They had started too late and they just couldn't move fast enough to keep up with the expansion.

And they didn't have enough ships.

Nothing had changed. Angie had so hoped it would have.

After the two hours, all eight chairmen met again in the *Star Mist* conference room and made sure all data were clear between all of them.

Then Angie suggested her idea that if the decision was to help in this fight, anyone who didn't want to remain should be allowed to board a Seeding vessel and return home.

Everyone agreed to that, but once again Gage said, "There has to be another way."

"Any way," Gina said.

"*Star Mist*," Gage said, "would you please show the edge of expansion of the alien race?"

The image came up showing the expansion and how the two other fleets were trying to stop it by wiping out galaxies, but clearly the galaxy they had just destroyed would have destroyed itself given time.

Suddenly Angie had an idea.

"If we stop the expansion," Angie said, "this race will collapse on itself and die. Correct?"

Everyone nodded and beside her Gage looked puzzled. "What are you thinking?"

"*Star Mist,*" Angie said, "please show the direction in arrows of the expansion from each galaxy that is still able to produce ships."

"Of course," Benny said as the arrows appeared. "We don't destroy the galaxy home worlds, we just stop their ships."

"The alien built ships have no defenses, do they?" Matt asked.

"None," Gage said. "They are just transports."

Angie was starting to get excited. She stared at the hologram of the galaxies around them.

"I can only extrapolate from the in-exact data we have at the moment," *Star Mist* said.

"We understand," Angie said. "Please try."

The arrows appeared coming from the leading edge galaxies and also the secondary edge galaxy. Behind that, the older occupied galaxies seemed to have no arrows.

"We are talking about millions and millions of alien ships in transit at any given time," Carrie said. "And we can't miss one ship or this all starts over again."

Matt nodded, then said, "Possibly. But we may have the time and the speed to get ahead of all this."

"Maybe," Gina said.

"*Star Mist*," Gage said, "from the information you have at the moment, could you give us an approximation of numbers of alien ships leaving galaxies over the next six months."

"I would need a lot more data," *Star Mist* said, "but with the data I have and the number of alien galaxies we know of, in six months over sixty million alien ships will leave the alien galaxies. That number, will, of course, increase rapidly if the ships reach their destinations and build more ships."

Angie didn't want to think about that number. Not until she had more information.

"*Star Mist*," Gage said, would you estimate the average transit time of an alien ship to a new galaxy?"

"Two years on average," *Star Mist* said. "These numbers are simply estimates from the best data, you understand.

"Yes, we understand," Gage said. "Thank you."

Angie looked directly at Ray and Tacita. "How many armed ships could we get here from human galaxies willing to help in this fight and how fast could we have them here?"

"We would have to convert ships to the new drive," Ray said, clearly thinking. "Then it would take nine to ten years at full new drive."

"Ten thousand ships would be a conservative number within twelve years and thousands more per year after that," Tacita said.

Ray nodded agreement.

Angie looked around. All of the chairmen were in deep thought.

"*Star Mist*," Angie said, "how many fighter ships are in The Exterminator and The Creator fleets combined?"

"Two thousand and ten confirmed," *Star Mist* said. "All with only standard trans-tunnel drive."

"*Star Mist*, how many ships do we have on board the three mother ships," Angie asked, "that are armed and capable of destroying an alien ship?"

"Nineteen hundred and sixty," *Star Mist* said.

Angie nodded.

"How many small fighting ships could the three mother ships build," Bennie asked, "and at what pace."

"Combined," *Star Mist* said, "the three mother ships are capable of building two military fighters a week each."

"Could that be increased if other resources were given to the task?" Gina asked. "And the fighters made much smaller?"

"Yes," *Star Mist* said. "If the fighters were small craft only capable of carrying ten crew members, each mother ship could produce upwards of twenty per week."

Angie could feel the excitement growing around the room.

"So if we stop the ships from leaving a galaxy," Benny said, "we then don't have to worry about the aliens left teeming in the galaxy. They will follow their own natural course of events."

"Exactly," Angie said. "We contain each galaxy and stay back and don't interfere, just as Seeders are supposed to do with alien galaxies."

Ray and Tacita were nodding in agreement.

"Damn," Benny said. "We need to find out if this will work because I am not at all up for destroying billions of lives and entire galaxies full of beings."

All of them agreed to that.

"So we meet in three hours," Angie said. "Dig in, find every detail we can and meet back here. Let's figure out ways to make this plan work."

All seven other chairmen nodded and a moment later she and Gage were back in their command chair letting *Star Mist* flow data at them as fast as possible.

THIRTY-EIGHT

GAGE WAITED WITH Angie in the conference room three hours later. Both of them were munching on sandwiches and Ray and Tacita were also eating at the other end of the table.

None of them spoke, mostly because there was nothing to say until all eight were in the room. Small talk just seemed way out of place at this point in time.

But Gage was feeling good about the chances Angie's idea might work.

They had come up with a couple of details that needed to be worked out to make this entire plan even have a chance

of working because it was something Carrie had said that haunted Gage's mind.

We can't miss a ship or all this starts over.

So he and Angie planned on bringing up some refinements that needed to be invented and invented quickly for this task at hand.

A few minutes later the other four arrived and all four went to a side table to take a sandwich and a bottle of water. None of them had even taken a few extra minutes to eat in the last three hours.

"Okay," Angie said, addressing the chairmen, "can we do this?"

"*Star Rain* believes our window of having this succeed is closing quickly," Gina said.

Gage nodded, as did everyone else. With this sort of exponential growth pattern, there was a point of no return that even faster ships and more ships would not be able to stop. And if that occurred, Gage had decided that the fallback plan was to set up a line of defense between the aliens and the human galaxies.

He doubted that would stop the flood for long, but it was better than having no secondary plan. But he had no intention of mentioning that plan to anyone at the moment.

"I see a few major problems," Benny said. "We will be unable in short order to staff the smaller fighters."

"We have a solution for that," Ray said. "Tacita and I can jump fighter crews from the Milky Way Galaxy here when that time comes."

"Perfect," Benny said, nodding.

"Thank you," Angie said.

Ray nodded.

Gage looked at Carrie and said, "You said something earlier that scares me to death."

Carrie nodded. "Can't miss a ship."

"Exactly," Gage said. "So we need scientists to develop a new scanning system that is long range and can pick up any alien ship signature."

"Extreme long range," Benny said, nodding.

"We can get the two inventors of the new trans-tunnel drive working on it at once back home," Tacita said.

"And many other scientists over thousands of planets as well," Ray said.

"And all the qualified scientists on all three ships need to go after that as well," Gage said. "That detail is critical."

"So do we have any sort of plan?" Matt asked.

"I do," Benny said after a moment. "Military thinking. *Star Mist,* would you show an image of the galaxies of the aliens, extrapolating from our current best information?"

Gage saw a light dome of galaxies. It was far more than he wanted to think about.

"This image is of the possible and likely alien galaxies in this area," *Star Mist* said. "If the alien expansion is moving in other directions, that information is not available."

Silence for a moment as everyone took in that detail. But Gage felt they had to focus on what they knew at the moment.

"Star Mist," Benny said, "please show a green area between unoccupied galaxies and the alien occupied galaxies."

The image expanded and a green dome appeared inside the arching mist of points of lights.

"First line of defense is along that green area," Benny said. "We try to stop every alien ship we can crossing into that green area."

"Star Mist," Angie said, "how many alien ships does it take to settle a galaxy?"

"One," *Star Mist* said.

Silence in the room again.

Gage just felt stunned.

"Star Mist, how long would that one ship take to populate the entire galaxy? Ray asked.

"One ship will take approximately ten thousand years to fill a Milky Way sized galaxy."

Everyone around the table nodded slowly.

"That green line is our first line of defense," Benny said. "We slow them down."

Gage stared at the simple illustration that showed them how impossible this task was considering how much space that green dome covered.

"We won't get them all," Benny said, "so our second line of defense is scout ships that are monitoring all the galaxies in this area for any sign of construction. If we can, we stop them before they start filling a galaxy and building more ships. If we can't, we isolate that galaxy and don't let any ship out."

Again more nodding.

Gage could see that this would work over a very long time. But did they have a long time was the question.

"Star Mist, would you please show a blue dome beyond all these galaxies illustrated?"

A blue dome, vast in size appeared beyond the hundreds of thousands of galaxies.

"Our third line of defense and why we need extreme long-range scanners. If any of their ships move past those galaxies or get out like that first ship that started all this, we need to have sensors out there that spot it."

Gage felt that would work and so did everyone else. But they were talking hundreds and hundreds of years, if not thousands.

"We are assuming these aliens are all going in one general direction," Angie said, bringing back up what *Star Mist* had mentioned. "We need to scout to see if there are more fronts on this battle besides this one."

"Agreed," Benny said.

Gage hated that, but he knew Angie was right and they didn't have enough information to know if this alien plague was spreading in only one general direction or in a complete circle. They basically only had the data they had gotten from the other human groups.

"Are we agreed on this plan in general?" Angie asked.

Every chairman in the room nodded.

"So what do we do about the other human groups?" Gage asked. He had no idea on this problem.

He looked around. Silence greeted him.

So Gage looked at Ray and Tacita directly. "Your suggestions? These two groups are clearly from your past and I would assume there is still bad blood."

Ray nodded and Tacita said nothing.

"Would they be worth our time in bringing them into this plan," Benny asked. "Their ships are no faster than the alien ships?"

Gage could see nothing but problems with even contacting them, but he said nothing.

"We let them do what they are doing," Angie said.

"I agree," Benny said.

"We don't hide from them," Carrie said.

"No hiding," Matt said, nodding.

"Damn right no hiding," Benny said. "We're out here cleaning up their mess. They started all this. Screw them."

Ray and Tacita both nodded and both looked slightly relieved.

"All right," Angie said. "One more thing. How about we set up some major ship factories in galaxies on that third line of defense?"

She looked at Tacita and Ray. "How fast could a major ship factory be set up on a planet on that third line of defense and how many large military craft could be built that would carry a hundred of the small fighters?"

"In essence," Gage said. "We are thinking small military mother ships to repair, transport, and so on."

"We will have that answer for you in one day," Ray said and Tacita nodded.

"That is a very good idea," Tacita said.

"Not one ship can get through," Carrie said. "We all need to remember that."

"And we all need to brief our entire crews on what is happening," Gage said.

"We do it at the same time twelve hours from now," Gina said.

"They all agreed.

"Let's get started," Angie said.

Gage looked directly at Ray and Tacita as they stood. "We need that extreme long-range scanner and we need it quickly."

Both nodded.

"And I have a hunch," Gage said, "if we are going to save humanity from its stupid mistake this time, every resource we have, not only from the Milky Way, but already Seeded galaxies will be needed in the fight."

Both again nodded.

"We will get every resource we can think of moving in this direction," Ray said.

He took Tacita's hand and they both vanished.

Gage glanced at Angie and she just nodded.

The decision had been made, but Gage knew it actually hadn't been a decision. A group of humans had made a mistake and their creation had gotten lose. Now for the sake of the known human universe, that mistake had to be stopped.

Gage hated that, but he knew it had to be done, no matter how long it took.

And he had no doubt this coming fight was going to take a very, very long time.

Centuries. But at the moment, he just couldn't think that far ahead.

THIRTY-NINE

FOR THREE SOLID days, the six chairmen worked and planned morning, noon and night, until it finally became clear to all of them that this fight was going to take years, decades, maybe even longer. Such a long time that Angie had a tough time even imagining.

And until someone invented a long-range scanner, they didn't even have any idea if they were winning or losing the fight. And Ray had told them it might take a decade for that breakthrough.

She wasn't sure if they had a decade, but they would do their best.

The weight of all this rested on the six of them. And Angie felt it every day. The image of how the aliens spread over the Milky Way galaxy haunted her night and day.

It was after a long meeting of the eight chairmen that Gage suggested to Angie they go to their quarters. He had mentioned to her that they needed to start getting into regular eating and sleeping routines and she had agreed. But so far, it hadn't been possible.

When they arrived, Angie was surprised to see that the table had been set with candles and dinner was staying warm in the oven. It smelled heavenly, like a fine Italian pasta and garlic bread.

"When did you have time to do this, mister?" she asked, turning to smile at Gage.

He laughed. "I asked for a little help from Soma and one of the ship's chefs."

Angie kissed him.

"We're staying in here for the evening," Gage said, smiling at her as he escorted her to her chair. "The known universe will have to get along without us for a short time."

She smiled as he put the wonderful-smelling pasta on the table and the garlic bread and then took his spot across from her.

In the living room, Miss Star, one of their now four cats noticed the food and got down from the back of the couch and came over beside the table.

Angie just stared at Gage's handsome beaming face and his wonderful green eyes. She never had gotten tired of doing that.

"So what's the occasion?" she asked

He pointed to the food. "Already forgotten our first meal together?"

She laughed, the memory of that first evening together in Portland flooding back in as clear as if had happened yesterday.

They had eaten exactly this same meal.

"Happy fifteen years from that first date," he said.

That surprised her. Had fifteen years really gone by? Wow, just wow.

He came around kissed her and she kissed him back.

No matter what was happening outside this apartment, they had each other and for that she couldn't be more grateful and happy.

Finally, before either of them broke their resolve and headed for the bedroom, Gage went back to his chair and they both dug into the food.

It was heavenly.

And just like the first night, the conversation over the food was fun and light and about anything but the fight with the alien expansion.

As they did on that first night, they ended up making passionate love after dinner.

Even after fifteen years, it was better than the first night.

She couldn't believe she had been with this wonderful man for that many years. Her memory was so clear of those first few days together, they seemed like yesterday.

And she remembered clearly that both of them had worried about their abilities to keep a long-term relationship going.

She could understand fifteen years. She wasn't sure about centuries, but she had a hunch the two of them would take that one year at a time.

But long term sure didn't seem like a problem anymore for either of them.

And as they lay there, holding each other, they talked about the wonderful fifteen years and their hope for far more than that.

Two cats joined them on the foot of the bed, wondering what she and Gage were doing, but not jumping down.

Gage mentioned how fast the years had passed and how happy he was and she agreed, adding in how happy she was that she wasn't aging.

And they laughed about how worried they both had been about a lasting relationship. It seemed so ironic to her now.

Finally, Angie turned and kissed him, then said, "Thank you?"

Three Seeders Universe Novels
Available at your favorite booksellers.

"The sex was that good?" he asked, pretending to be shocked.

She laughed. "Yes, thank you for that, but thank you more for this wonderful surprise evening and remembering our first night. I needed to be reminded why we are here doing what we are doing."

He nodded, then said simply, "I needed the reminder as well."

"So, let's make sure we mark every year with something special," she said.

"To keep us grounded."

"Grounded in a spaceship with over a million people under our command," she said, smiling. "Yeah, that kind of grounded."

He laughed and just shook his head to that.

After a moment, she raised up and looked at him. "If memory serves, which it does just fine, we made love twice that first night."

"That was pure sex," he said. "I fell in love with you long before that night following you around in the wilds of the mountains."

She laughed and agreed that the first night had been wonderful, pure passionate sex.

"So lieutenant, are you up for a second round this evening?" she asked after a moment.

"You know I'm over four hundred years old, don't you?" he said, looking into her eyes.

"So I take that as a yes," she said, looking into his deep green eyes.

"Hell, yes," he said.

And she giggled like a young girl as he moved toward her, scattering cats to the floor.

And for the first time in years, she felt young again.

Coming Next Month
Star Rain: A Seeders Universe Novel

Three Cold Poker Gang Novels
Available at your favorite booksellers.

#1... October 2013

#2... November 2013

#3... December 2013

#4... January 2014

#5... February 2014

#6... March 2014

#7... April 2014

#8... May 2014

#9... June 2014

#10... July 2014

#11... August 2014

#12...September 2014

#13...October 2014

#14...November 2014

#15...December 2014

#16...January 2015

#17...February 2015

#18...March 2015

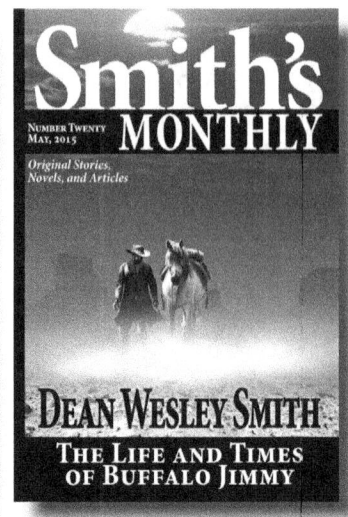

Now Available
from all your favorite booksellers in trade paper and electronic editions.

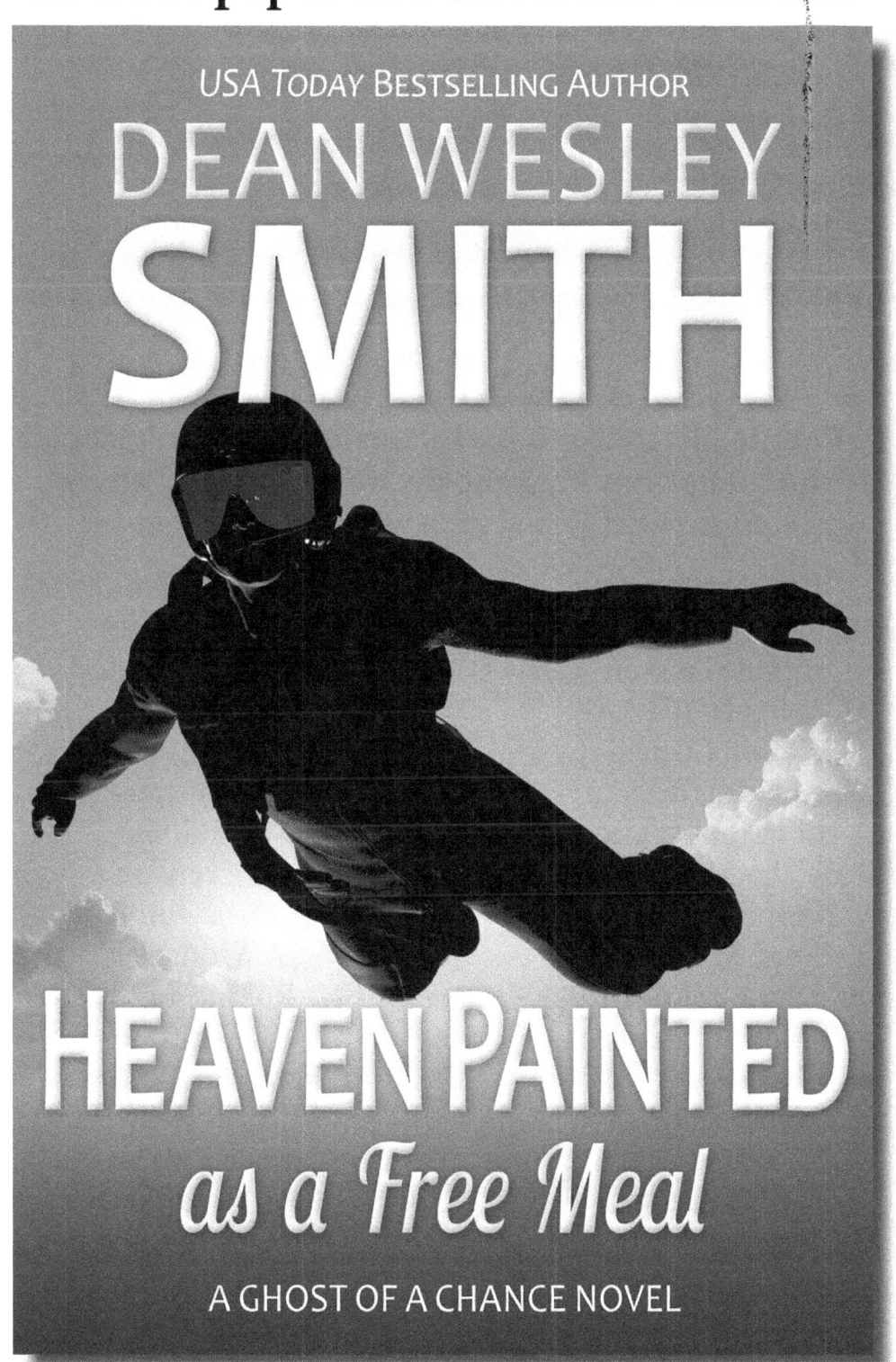

USA TODAY BESTSELLING AUTHOR

DEAN WESLEY
SMITH

HEAVEN PAINTED
as a Free Meal

A GHOST OF A CHANCE NOVEL

Thank You!!

I would like to thank the following wonderful people who support my blog and my work through Patreon. Your support is very important to me. Thanks!

Irette Y. Patterson

Chris Cousino

Jane Lawson

Shantnu Tiwari

Rob Cornell

Erick Lindman

Christopher Ridge

Miguel Angel Alonso Pulido

Nancy Hendrickson

Ryan M. Williams

Jacob Proffitt

Marian Goldeen

Brenda Bergeron

John Connelly

Gary Speer

Megan Bryce

Michelle Tatam

Ann Tucker

Kari Wolfe

Terry Mixon

James Husun

Kathryn Rooney

Sherman Cox

Chong Go

Maria Grace

Grondpom

Fen

Livia Quinn

Amri Ackers

Robin Brande

J.R. Murdock

Kathleen McClure

Michael Kelberer

Gunnar Gunderson

F.I. Goldhaber

Mary Jo Rabe

John Kilgallon

Dave Hendrickson

www.ingramcontent.com/pod-product-compliance
Lightning Source LLC
Chambersburg PA
CBHW081151170626
46813CB00009B/3155